"This was a great book! I loved the adventures of Grace and her watermelon family. It's an easy and fun read."

—KRISTY CARDINAL
Illiana Watermelon Promotion's Coordinator 2000-2008
Past Illiana Watermelon Queen 1998
Present member of Illiana Watermelon Association and
National Watermelon Association

"As a former National Watermelon Queen, I loved reminiscing about my year and vicariously living through Grace. I couldn't put the book down!"

—MAGGIE BAILEY
2009 National Watermelon Queen

"The author provides a captivating romance novel of the tragedy of life and the misplaced trust of the heart that seeks love. The heroin (Grace) finds true love and her first kiss in the only place she had not looked—right before her eyes."

—BARB HELM
Miss Indiana Board Member and Field Director

APRIL SMITH

Ambassador International
GREENVILLE. SOUTH CAROLINA & BELFAST, NORTHERN IRELAND

www.ambassador-international.com

Loving Grace

ISBN: 978-1-62020-619-5
eISBN: 978-1-62020-629-4

Printed in the United States of America | First Edition
Cover Design and Page Layout by Hannah Nichols
eBook Conversion by Anna Riebe Raats

Ordering Information:
Quantity sales. Special discounts are available on quantity purchases by corporations, associations, and others. For details, contact the publisher at the address below or by emailing sales@emeraldhouse.com.

AMBASSADOR INTERNATIONAL
Emerald House
411 University Ridge, Suite B14
Greenville, SC 29601, USA
www.ambassador-international.com

AMBASSADOR BOOKS
The Mount
2 Woodstock Link
Belfast, BT6 8DD, Northern Ireland, UK
www.ambassadormedia.co.uk

The colophon is a trademark of Ambassador

To Grandma Jan

Chapter 1

I'M LATE. THE PHONE IS already ringing off the wall by the time I make it to my desk. I toss my keys and bag to the side, not really bothering with where they land. I'll get them later. I grab the phone and snag the corner of the desk with my hip. That's going to leave a mark. "Melon Ridge Farms. How may I help you?" I ask, hopping around and rubbing the spot.

The phone call doesn't take long. I take a message and write *John Baron* at the top of the memo pad. The name pretty much sums it up. He is the largest melon farmer in the Midwest. Mr. Baron is great, though.

I notice an envelope with my name on it, but I set it aside. I have to get the orders going first.

I'm about an hour in when the door slams open. I stifle a groan and keep my eyes on my papers. It's Beau Baron—one of the boss' sons. The worst part of my job is having to deal with him on a daily basis.

He leans against the doorframe, just watching me. I stop and raise an eyebrow.

"Is there something I can help you with?" I look at him pointedly, hoping he'll take the hint and go back out the door he came in through.

"Dad's wondering why you haven't called him," he mumbles.

He looks out the window like he would rather be anywhere but in here.

"Call him?" I use the same bored voice he used.

"He left you a note in an envelope. He got worried when you didn't call right away," he explains.

"I will now. Thanks." Trying to get rid of him, I add, "You can go now."

"I'm supposed to wait for you," he says with an air of boredom.

The call to Mr. Baron makes my insides churn. I need to meet him at the packing shed and read the note on the way. Unfortunately for me, Beau will bring me in the pick-up truck. I brace myself for the ride to the shed. Why couldn't it have been Bennett, Beau's older brother? Bennett is funny and not at all like Beau. I've been crushing on Bennett Baron since seventh grade. He makes it pretty easy to do so with his southern charm and boyish good looks.

Beau is already waiting at the door. He opens the rusted, red door, and we head out in the hot June sun.

"Do you know what this is about?"

"Read the letter, but don't shoot the messenger," he says.

I tear through the envelope—a million terrible thoughts drumming through my head.

It's worse than I thought. Mr. Baron has signed me up for the watermelon queen pageant. He's the president of the Midwest Watermelon Association, and he has chosen to sponsor me. In other words, I'm competing in a pageant to win the title of Midwest Watermelon Queen. I crumple the paper and close my eyes. *Breathe,* I remind myself.

"Well, say something," Beau says.

"It's not a good idea," I whisper and then exhale.

"Saying something or the pageant?"

"Both." I stop. "Wait a minute. You knew?"

Beau frowns a little bit, but that's all the answer I get.

What in the world was Mr. Baron thinking? The watermelon family who sponsors an individual knows that if their candidate wins, they are in charge of taking them to all the promotions. The organization pays for all of the expenses; but the person who sponsored the queen is basically her guardian for a year, and the queen's schedule is non-stop. Fun and exciting, but non-stop. He knows that Beau and I are like two roosters in a hen house. We're always fighting. Spending an entire year in each other's presence doesn't sound like a good idea.

"Did you tell him it was a bad idea?" I ask.

"Of course, I did. Do you think I want to spend an entire year carting you and your stuff around?" He glances over, annoyance clearly written on his face.

"Well, at least you're honest. Don't worry; the feeling is mutual."

"Grace, that's not what I meant," he says, trying to backpedal.

"Save it." I turn away, irritated.

We used to be different before Luke died, but in the eighth grade, things changed. Finally, the truck pulls up to the packing shed, so I swing the door open before it even comes to a full stop, making my way to Mr. Baron. He's talking with a semi driver as the last few melons are loaded into the trailer. He gives the man a handshake and makes his way toward me with a smile on his face.

"I see Beau got you here in one piece," Mr. Baron remarks.

"Yes, sir. Thanks for having him bring me over."

Mr. Baron smiles, making it obvious why he usually gets what he wants. He has a way about him that makes it hard to say no.

"Well, Miss Grace, is your answer yes?"

I take a breath to harden myself. "Mr. Baron, first, I want to thank you for the opportunity, but I don't—"

He interrupts.

"Keep in mind that if you were to win, every event you go to is paid for—your clothing, travel expenses—not to mention you get paid per promotion. And you will have the opportunity to compete for the national queen title in a year."

I had forgotten about that. The queen is well-cared-for, and she is paid, too. I could really use that money for college. Plus, the traveling would be so much fun. I'm pretty enough. I have no problem talking in front of crowds, and I know most of the people involved with the Midwest Watermelon Association because I've been working for Mr. Baron these last few years.

"I'll do it," I blurt out before I can change my mind.

"Thanks, Grace. No need to come into the office tomorrow. Pamela will pick you up in the morning to do whatever you ladies need done before the convention this weekend. She's been after me for weeks to get you to do this. With only Bennett and Beau and no daughter to sponsor . . . well she pretty much told me not to come home tonight unless I had the answer she wanted."

He leaves me standing there. I hadn't thought about Mrs. Baron being involved in this. I should have known it was her idea. She was the Southwest Watermelon Queen thirty years ago, and to hear her tell it, it was one of the best years of her life. My stomach starts to feel like I've drunk too much water after working in the sun all morning. I swallow back the nausea and head to the truck. When he sees me, Beau closes the tailgate of the truck. Then he meets me at the passenger side door.

"From the look on your face, I'd say Dad got his way."

I don't respond. There's no reason. I climb in the cab, and Beau shuts the door.

He walks around the front of the truck, shaking a few workers' hands as he passes by.

He starts the truck and turns the air on full blast. Even with the windows rolled down, it's still suffocating in the cab.

"Why couldn't you have been a girl?" I grumble.

"Really, Grace? I think that's one you'll have to figure out on your own. Or maybe you want to ask my parents how that all works."

"Funny." I roll my eyes. "You know what I mean."

Seriously, he is so annoying. I don't know why I even bother trying to talk to him.

"Yeah, I do, but I don't think I'd look very good in a dress, do you?" The smirk on his face says he is enjoying this too much.

"I don't think your ego can handle what I think," I say, looking out the window.

The truck comes to a stop in front of the office.

"You know you like me. All the girls do." He wiggles his brow, trying to be funny.

"Not this girl," I shoot back, hopping out of the truck.

He chuckles.

I don't look back, but I yell over my shoulder, "Even so, it wouldn't hurt you to at least act humble, Beau Baron."

I close the office door behind me and slowly breathe out through my nose. Closing my eyes, I lean against the door trying to shut out the conversation Beau and I just had. When I'm calm enough to open my eyes again, I see the answering machine blinking, and now I am an hour behind on my paperwork. My bag and keys are still where I left them. I stand them back up and take a breath. I do want to be the watermelon queen. I'm sure I won't have to see Beau that much. If I win, it will be Mr. and Mrs. Baron taking me to most of the events anyway. Right now, though, I need to put my thoughts aside and tackle the work that is piling up on the desk.

I've been making headway with the messages and stacks of orders for the better part of four hours when the door opens.

"Just as I suspected, Grace," Mrs. Baron says airily. "You didn't stop to eat."

Mrs. Baron—Pamela to most—is always smiling. She's your stereotypical southern girl—light and breezy on the outside, nerves of steel on the inside. Mr. Baron was probably telling the truth when he said he wouldn't be welcomed home if he didn't get a yes out of me.

"I'm doing all right, Mrs. Baron." I point to the wrapper of the granola bar I had consumed earlier.

"Nonsense. I brought you some watermelon salsa and a chicken salad sandwich," she says, laying the plate on my desk.

"Thanks." My mouth begins to water as soon as she sets the food in front of me.

Mrs. Baron can cook. No one turns down anything she brings to the table—and for good reason.

"You eat, and I'll talk," she commands.

I nod my agreement as I slide the tomato back into the sandwich.

"Tomorrow, I will pick you up at nine in the morning. I've already set up an appointment at Glam to pick out a dress. From there, we will take care of your interview and speech outfit. Oh, and we'll need something for the cocktail party, too."

"Okay," I say in between bites.

She puts her hand on my shoulder.

"Thanks, Grace," she says, tearing up. "Well, with your mother gone and me with only Bennett and Beau, you've made me very happy. She was my best friend, you know?"

"Yes, ma'am, I know," I say, swallowing the lump in my throat.

Then, in true southern fashion, she blinks her eyes a couple of times and turns back into her bright, sunshiny self.

"I don't mean to keep you. I'll be on my way," she says. "Just start thinking about your speech."

And then she's out the door.

I swallow to force the sandpapery dryness away and breathe. Taking two deep breaths, I focus on the work that I still need to get done, and I finish the last stack of paperwork right at five. I barely had time to finish the orders for today, let alone think about my speech. I switch the answering machine back on and check that the back door is locked before heading home to Gramps.

The screen door makes its normal protests as I open it. The house smells like meatloaf and roses.

"Gramps?" I call out.

I hear his muffled reply coming from the kitchen. "In here."

"I put your meatloaf in. Should be ready in a few minutes." He leans against the counter in my grandma's old, frilly, floral apron.

I sit at the countertop, drumming my fingers.

"Sounds good." I try to sound upbeat, but I'm unable to hide the tremble in my voice.

"Spill it. What's got you down, Short Stack?"

I let it all pour out. Mrs. Baron pretty much mandating that I do the pageant. My fear of looking like an idiot. My frustration at myself because I can do this. I'm a good public speaker, and I love watermelon and the people in the watermelon association. They've been good to me, too, this past year, with everything that I've had happen. Then, I start rambling about traveling and leaving Gramps behind.

Gramps lets me go until I have it all out. He even managed to get the meatloaf out during my little verbal rain shower.

"So, what I'm hearing is a lot of excuses, Short Stack. Sounds like, to me, you are letting fear get in the way. Let's talk about it over supper, and we can pray about it, too."

Gramps puts the meatloaf on the table, and we make quick work of filling our plates. After we thank God for our food, Gramps prays over the decision I'll need to make about competing for the Midwest Watermelon Queen. A feeling of safety and calm washes over me as we take the matter to the Lord.

Chapter 2

THE CONCIERGE TAKES ONE LOOK at all of our bags and signals for another bellhop. Mrs. Baron does not travel light. To be fair, we are here for three days, and there are many events taking place that will require clothing changes—or so I've been told. My suitcase is stuffed so full, it's bulging around the zipper. I cross my fingers, hoping it won't spring open as the bellhop maneuvers it onto the cart. And while this weekend is about me "garnering attention" (Mrs. Baron's words, not mine), I don't think my clothes flying out of my suitcase in the entrance is the type of attention she's hoping for.

"Grace, you come with me and John to get you checked in. Bennett and Beau, you two follow the bellhop up to our rooms," Mrs. Baron says.

"Good luck, Grace," Bennett says before he and Beau head toward the elevator.

"Thanks." I stand there, watching them walk away.

Bennett and Beau—now there are two boys who couldn't be more alike, yet different. Both are tall, dark-haired, broad-shouldered, Christian boys. But where Bennett is kind and funny, Beau is rude and, well, rude. Bennett is in his second year of college; he's studying edaphology, but we just call him the dirt doctor for short. Beau is

15

a senior in high school, and he studies anything besides his school books. I shake my head to bring myself back to reality and head over to the front desk.

Check-in is a breeze. It takes all of five minutes to give my name and get our schedule for the weekend.

"I'm so excited for you, Grace," Mrs. Baron says.

We make our way to the elevator. The first item on the competition agenda is a meet-and-greet with the judges and contestants. Then we go directly on to give our speeches.

"It's very important to make a good first impression," she reminds me.

She looks like a five-year-old who was just given permission to eat all of the cookies in the cookie jar. I stifle a sigh and follow Mr. and Mrs. Baron into the elevator. The ride takes less than a minute, but Mrs. Baron spends the entire time giving me her version of a pep talk about who is who and helping me connect the judges with the different businesses we work with.

When we finally stop in front of our suite, my brain is on information overload. Mr. Baron opens the door and steps back. "Ladies," he says, motioning for us to enter.

Ornate is the only word I can think of that does the rooms justice. "Wow, this is beautiful."

"Your room is over here, Grace." Mrs. Baron does the honors of showing me to my room. The cream and taupe décor is soothing. It does a lot for my nerves. My suitcases are already stacked along one wall, waiting for me to unpack them.

"We are across the hall, and the boys are on the other side of the living room," Mrs. Baron says. "I'll leave you to unpack."

Dressed and ready thirty minutes early, I give Gramps a call.

"Hello?"

"Hey, Gramps, it's me."

"Hi, Short Stack. How's it going?"

"Well, I look the part. Mrs. Baron has me all dressed up." I try to make my voice sound light and airy because I'm trying to hide from Gramps the fact that my stomach is tied up in knots. And to be fair, the dress is stunning.

It's a green, halter top dress that flairs out to the knees. At the waist, there are large, emerald green stones that circle around to the back of the dress. I have on large, emerald green earrings and a bangle to match. My hair is down in soft curls with one side pulled back with an emerald rhinestone comb.

"And?" Gramps asks.

He can always tell when I have more to say but don't want to say it.

"I'm nervous. I don't know if I should be doing this. Mom, Dad . . ." I pause, fighting back tears. "Luke," I barely whisper.

"Grace," Gramps says, using that voice adults reserve for little children or scared animals. "You're going to be fine. Don't let the past stop you. God has plans for you."

"I know, but how do I live when they aren't anymore?"

"It was an accident, Short Stack. You've got to let it go and live."

"I'm trying Gramps." I try to sound strong, but my voice only comes out wobbly.

"I know you are. I love you. I'll be praying for you the whole time you give that speech."

"Thank you, Gramps. I'll let you know how it goes when I'm done."

"You won't have to. Mrs. Baron has been blowing up my phone with text message after text message about you already," he says, unable to hide the frustration in his voice.

I laugh my first genuine laugh in the last forty-eight hours.

"See, I told you, you'd love that new phone."

"Ha. The only things I love are the Lord, you, and your grandma's lasagna. In that order, too, mind you, girl," he says gruffly.

But I can imagine the smile on his face and the creases around his eyes as he talks.

"I love you, Gramps. You were just what I needed."

I hang up the phone and head toward the living room. Mrs. Baron is perched on the ottoman, talking with Bennett.

"Grace, you look lovely, dear." And without even taking a breath, she goes on. "Let's get a move on. We need to make those judges fall in love with you."

"Pretty easy to do in that dress," Bennett says with a wink.

He offers his arm.

Looping my arm in his, I tease him back. "Your flattery won't work here, Bennett Baron. I'm on to you."

We make it to the meet-and-greet before I'm ready, but at least the expression on my face is natural. Bennett was telling me all kinds of funny stories from his last semester.

"We'll leave you here," Mrs. Baron says.

I nod.

"Just remember to make the connections with everyone I told you about."

"Mom, you're making her nervous," Bennett says, thankfully interrupting anything else she was going to say.

"We'll see you in the conference room for your speech," Mrs. Baron says.

I give them a thumb's up and head into what is supposed to be finger foods and light conversation. What I find is each girl working the room and chatting with each judge individually. It's like that trash TV speed dating show, where everyone gets five minutes with their possible date, and then they have to switch. People on the show are aggressive and pushy—only it's worse than that in here. I fight the urge to become a wallflower and head over to the first available judge I see.

"Hi. I'm Grace Summer." I grin before offering my hand for a handshake.

"Hi, Grace. I'm Tony Williams." He takes my hand.

"So, what area of the industry are you in?"

"I work for Inlake Containers, which makes the boxes the melon farmers use to pack their produce," he says.

"Ah. Which one? The Barons use the one out of Evansville. I was on the phone just the other day ordering more boxes for the farm."

We chat, and I make the connection with him that Mrs. Baron told me to. I tell him what I do for Mr. Baron, and the conversation stays on the watermelon business, which is great. I can talk watermelon with the best of them. Before long, Amy, another contestant, comes along. I make my farewell to judge number one and head on to the next one.

The time ticks by as I go through the same "getting-to-know-you" ritual and make a connection with each one, so they'll remember me. By the time the two hours are over, I'm buzzing with ideas to use in the office on Monday. I head straight to Mr. Baron as soon as I can to tell him what I've learned.

He's in the convention center, sitting at the table with Mrs. Baron, Bennett, and Beau. I walk over to the table to join them. Bennett hops up to pull my chair out for me.

"Thanks." Before I can say anything else, Mrs. Baron is peppering me with questions about the meet-and-greet.

"How did it go?"

"I think it went okay. I talked about everything you told me to, and then I told them that I worked for Mr. Baron in the office."

"You talked about office work with them?"

"Yes, ma'am."

Suddenly, I feel like I've done something wrong, and Mrs. Baron's face agrees with me.

"Well, that's great. You know all about the business side. Let them see what a good head you have on your shoulders," Mr. Baron says.

"True. But I would rather you have been able to just make small talk," Mrs. Baron says.

"I did that, too." I swallow, then add, "I think I made you proud, Mrs. Baron."

"Oh, Grace, of course you did. I mean, just look at you—bright, beautiful, talented. I'm already proud of you. Your mom would be, too. Boys, tell her how beautiful she is."

"You know what I think of you in that dress, Miss Grace," Bennett says, putting on a funny southern accent.

I laugh, unable to take him seriously.

"Beau?" Mrs. Baron prompts him.

Beau is like one of those puppies that fails obedience school over and over again. No matter how hard Mrs. Baron tries, manners just don't seem to stick to Beau Baron.

"You do look pretty today," he says, making eye contact and then quickly looking back to this weekend's itinerary pamphlet.

"Thanks." I try not to roll my eyes at his insincerity.

I'm saved from having to say more when Kristen, the queen program coordinator, collects me for our speeches. "Good luck" comes from around the table, except from Beau, who looks like he swallowed part of a watermelon rind.

We wait in the hall, listening for the claps that signal the end of another speech, which puts us closer to our turns to go. There are ten of us total. I happen to be contestant number ten. Mrs. Baron said something about saving the best for last; but all I can think about is that all too soon, I'm going to be up there. I run through my speech one more time. This is the one thing that I wouldn't let Mrs. Baron put her hands on. I know this industry. I've worked it every summer for the last five years. Besides, Gramps is praying for me.

I offer up a small prayer of my own. *God, I don't know what You have planned for me. If I'm supposed to win, then help me to be worthy of the title. If I'm not supposed to win, that's okay, too. Just please don't let me forget my speech in front of everyone, Lord.*

I finish just as the applause signals the end of contestant number nine's speech. The door opens, and I make my way to the podium. The walk seems longer with everyone's eyes trained on me.

I stand at the podium and look out at the crowd. A calmness washes over me as I give my speech.

"Ladies and Gentlemen, I want to take this time to thank you for your hard work and dedication to the watermelon industry. I remember as a little girl following my brother over to play with his best friend at Melon Ridge Farms. The Barons were always so kind and welcoming. The boys would put up with me, while we worked turning vines or setting the melons in the fields. But it was there on that farm that I fell in love. I fell in love with the watermelon world. It's where I put in hours hauling melons onto wagons and driving the tractor, only so I could pick the radio station that I knew drove the boys crazy."

I stop for a breath, and the audience laughs at my joke. "I understand the long hours and back-breaking labor you put into it each and every day. How do I know? Well, because I'm lucky enough to still work for Mr. Baron. Only now, I am his secretary, which means for the last couple of years, I've had the pleasure to be here with you in a working capacity. However, this year, I stand on the other side of the podium, asking for the chance of a lifetime. Please consider me, Grace Summer, for Miss Midwest Watermelon Queen. Thanks a melon for your time."

I step back from the podium, and the room erupts into applause. I give a mega-watt smile and chance a look over at Mrs. Baron. If her smile were any bigger, her face would split in half. It's safe to say that I did a good job. I'm shipped off to my room, like the rest of the contestants, with the promise of room service. Tomorrow will be a long day, and I'm beat, anyway. All I really want is a long soak in the tub and a cheeseburger.

After three of the longest but most enjoyable days I've had in a while, the moment is here. Kristen calls all of the contestants to the stage. I will either find myself with a crown on my head and a summer full of traveling the country or with a stack of wagon orders to fill come Monday. I can't believe the butterflies—no, scratch that, hippos—that are dancing around in my stomach. There really wasn't any time to get to know the girls, so I can't say who stands the best chance of winning. When the applause dies down, Kristen takes to the stage to make her announcement.

"Ladies and Gentlemen, your new Miss Midwest Watermelon Queen is . . . Grace Summer."

Did I hear her right? One look at Mrs. Baron lets me know for sure I heard my name. She has her hand linked with Mr. Baron's and is jumping up and down. The whole left side of his body looks like a pogo stick bouncing out of control. I step forward and wait for the crown and sash. Cameras are flashing all around me. The crown and sash in place, I take my first walk as queen. Next, it's the judges and board members for pictures. Mr. and Mrs. Baron follow for their turn. She hugs me. Then, she hugs me again.

"I knew you could do it! This year is going to be the best," she says.

The boys fall in line next for pictures. I'm blinded from all the snapshots. I step back a little, trying to regain focus, and snag my heel on my dress. I careen to one side.

"Careful," Beau says, grabbing my arm to steady me.

"Sorry, the flashes blinded me."

He frowns and says, "You better get used to it. Mom is sure to document every moment of your queen tour this year."

"Too true." I scrunch up my face.

After about eight hundred more flashes, Kristen finally calls the photo shoot to a halt and ushers us to a small meeting room, where I'll sign a contract. She gives a quick rundown of the contract, which can be summed up with "don't do anything dumb on social media," "don't be late for promotions," and "don't ever, under any circumstances, go out alone while on promotions or trips."

She goes on to explain what all she will be coordinating for us. Mrs. Baron is given the upcoming travel schedule. We will be headed to Texas at the end of the week for the final convention and queen crowning. I will get to meet the other queens from the surrounding organizations. But before that, there will be a homecoming event with the newspaper. They want to follow me and the Barons around while we work on the farm. That sounds easy enough.

We head back to the convention center to find Bennett and Beau. My first official duty as queen is to start off the watermelon ball with a waltz. Earlier today, all the contestants got a crash course in waltzing. Some girls were quick studies. Me? Not so much. I made Bennett practice with me for another hour before I felt comfortable following the waltz dance pattern. I look for Bennett, but Beau is waiting for me instead.

"He's busy being the dirt doctor," he says while offering me his hand. "I told him I'd fill in."

I give him my hand and let him lead me to the dance floor, trying not to panic. I felt comfortable with Bennett. He would have helped me through the steps.

"Try not to step on my foot like you did in sixth grade," he says, while we take our positions and wait for the music to start.

"Uck, it was you who stepped on my foot," I remind him just as the music starts, and Beau whisks me across the dance floor.

"Either way, lucky for you, Mom made me learn how to waltz last winter before Dad became the association's president."

After a few strands, everyone joins us on the dance floor. The night is meant to be magical with the fancy lighting and decorations. I try to ignore who I'm dancing with and catalog everything instead. That way, I can tell Gramps about it tomorrow, since he's the only one I have left to tell about my day. It hurts to think about it. My insides start feeling like they're being squeezed and twisted. There's still a big part of me that feels guilty for having fun. I fight to keep the happy expression on my face, but it's a losing battle. Beau's rude remark and the pain of loss hits me in waves, threatening to drag me under.

"Don't do that," Beau says.

"Do what?" I ask.

"Let's get a drink." He leads me off the dance floor.

"You have to stop feeling guilty, Grace," Beau says.

"That's not what I'm doing."

"Yes, you are. I can see it in your face."

"It's harder than it sounds."

He rubs his neck. "I'm sure it is. But if you think for one second that your parents would want you missing out—"

"Just don't."

He closes his mouth before he can say anything else and leans against the wall. I blink my eyes, trying to control the tears.

"I'm sorry. I shouldn't be lecturing you. This is your night, right?"

He lets out a slow breath and puts his hands on his hips. He looks angry, like my meltdown is all my fault, but I'm too busy trying not to cry to fight.

"It is, but your mother may be enjoying it more than me right now." I point to Mrs. Baron, who is talking a mile a minute to Kristen, the queen coordinator. I can't help but feel a little deflated.

"Probably," he says.

He offers me his arm. I take it and work at enjoying the moment. We head back toward the dance floor and Bennett. Beau deposits me in his capable arms, clearly happy to be rid of me, and, for a few minutes, I get to imagine what dancing with Bennett would feel like if he knew how into him I really am.

I spend the entire night dancing with one gentleman after another. It seems everyone wants to get to know the new Midwest Watermelon Queen. When the ball is over, I can't feel my feet, but I feel like I've accomplished what I needed to. I know most of the people who make up the watermelon organization. Hopefully, I was able to put a good word in for Mr. Baron with the melon buyers, too.

Chapter 3

WE ARE ASSEMBLED IN FRONT of the hothouse, our name for the greenhouse, in the back of the shed. The news crew has been setting up for the last few minutes. Mrs. Baron has her boys—all three of them—assembled and dressed for the broadcast. She is picking off invisible pieces of lint from Mr. Baron's shirt. I smooth down my red, bell-shaped skirt with my sweaty palms. The nerves are worse than I thought they'd be.

"Grace, stop that. You will do just fine," Mrs. Baron says.

She adjusts the collar on my white, sleeveless blouse, while I mess with the black belt. Apparently, she isn't as relaxed as she'd have us to believe. She can't stop nitpicking.

Stormy Meryweather walks up, mic in her hand.

"Okay, guys," she starts to give us a quick rundown of what to expect for the interview but stops mid-sentence when she gets the go from her camera man. "We are going live in five, four, three, two . . . We are here today with newly-crowned Midwest Watermelon Queen, Grace Summer. So, tell me, Grace, how has it been so far?"

She points the mic toward my face.

"Well, it's been a whirlwind. I'm blessed to have known the Barons my whole life. I've had the opportunity to work in the fields and, now, in the office for Mr. Baron. With my new title, I can't wait to represent the watermelon organization."

Stormy flashes her dimples at the camera and then asks, "What's on the agenda first for you?"

"Up next, I get to attend the Southern Watermelon Convention. I can't wait to see who the lucky girl will be."

"And will the whole Baron family attend with you?" she asks.

Mr. Baron takes that one. "We plan to attend as many promotions together as we can; but sometimes the farm will need me, and I'll send Mrs. Baron and the boys with Grace. In short, it will be a family affair as often as it can be."

"And what do you boys say to following this lovely young lady around?" she asks.

"It's an honor to be able to escort the watermelon queen to her promotions. Plus, with Dad about to become the national watermelon president, we all know we'll need to pull our weight more than ever," Bennett says.

A worker stands behind Stormy with some soil samples in his hands. He looks expectantly at Bennett.

"Speaking of pulling our own weight, it looks like I'm needed now. Excuse me." Bennett politely leaves the interview and walks over to the worker.

"Mrs. Baron, this one's for you. Each girl must have a sponsor to be a part of the queen competition. What made you choose Grace?"

"It's like Grace said, we've known her from the time she was a little girl. She and her brother used to come and play. Then, when they were older, they worked in the fields with Beau," Mrs. Baron says.

Stormy looks at Beau and asks, "Well, Beau, what do you think of your childhood friend now? How has she changed?"

My stomach drops a little bit. I shoot him a look that says, *please don't say anything embarrassing.*

"Well, she's taller than she used to be, but she still listens to terrible music. My advice would be to get to the radio before she does."

I'm going to strangle him. I keep the smile on my face and put my hands behind my back to keep Stormy and the general population from seeing me clench my fists. It's not the image I want portrayed on the evening news.

Beau continues, "But on a serious note, she will be an excellent representative for our industry. My entire family and hers are very proud of her."

Now, why did he go on to say that?

"Thanks, Beau," Stormy says. Then she asks, "Anything you'd like to add, Grace?"

"I just want to say that I will continue to work very diligently for the watermelon industry. I have already come to love the people who make up our organization. I want to thank Mr. and Mrs. Baron for all they have done for me, and, lastly, I can't wait to see what this year holds for me."

Stormy turns to the camera.

"It looks like Grace is set for a melon load of fun this year. This is Stormy Meryweather, signing off for Channel 44 news."

The cameraman quickly packs up his gear, carting it back to the news van.

"You guys were great," Stormy says.

"Beau, the crowd is going to love what you said about Grace." She winks at me.

"Yes, thank you, Beau. You always were such a charmer," I say, while strangling him with my eyes.

He just smirks and winks at me.

"Mrs. Baron, if I could talk to you for a bit. I think this is going to be a hit. The station may want to do several follow-up stories. Maybe we could chat about a possible timeline?" Stormy asks.

Mrs. Baron beams with excitement. "Yes, that's a great idea," she says, while following Stormy to the van.

"But, Mrs. Baron, the newspaper reporter is coming up the drive," I point to the little silver car headed toward us.

"You and Beau will have to do it," Mrs. Baron says over her shoulder.

"Mom, I need to get back to the fields," Beau protests.

"Nonsense, you can't leave Grace alone," Mrs. Baron says without even looking back.

It's a lost cause. We are stuck together for better or worse.

"Let's just get this done," Beau grumbles in resignation.

We walk over to the reporter.

Her handshake is firm. "Morgan Jones," she introduces herself.

We make quick introductions and then basically go through the same question-and-answer pattern from before. Only this time, I talk into an audio recorder. Beau stands to one side and lets me do most of the talking, which is smart on his part. After what he said to the news station reporter, if he so much as made one move to answer a question, I would have stomped on his foot for real this time—no matter what his story about sixth grade is.

"Okay, I've got enough for the write-up. I just need some photos. Is there a watermelon field we can get some pictures in?" Morgan asks.

"Yes, ma'am. I know the perfect place," Beau says.

"Let me just grab my boots," I throw over my shoulder as I head to grab them from the office. "I don't think these heels would last very long in the field."

Beau is already waiting in the beat-up pickup truck when I hop in.

"Morgan's going to follow us. I need to check the irrigation system when she's done taking photos," Beau says.

The truck makes a chugging sound as the engine turns over, but she starts up.

"That sounds bad," I say, stating the obvious.

"Yup, probably going to die for good soon," he replies, without taking his eyes off the road.

"Speaking of the death of things, I know someone who might find themselves in the same condition of the truck. Why did you say that on TV about me?"

"It was funny."

"Hilarious."

"And the other part is good publicity for the farm and you. Just playing my part."

He reaches to change the radio station, but I beat him to it.

"I don't think so. Not after what you said on the news about my music tastes. You'll just have to suffer."

I crank the radio up and let what Beau calls "girlie music" blast through the cab.

"This is terrible music," he complains.

I act like I can't hear him. "Sorry, music's too loud," I yell back, pointing to my ears, then shrugging.

The mile-and-a-half drive doesn't take very long. But the sun is close to setting; the clouds are getting dark; and it looks like it's raining a ways off.

Morgan is all business when it comes to getting the shots she wants. She has me by the watermelons, turning the vines. Then she adds Beau in. She takes what seems like a million pictures. I'm not going to lie—my favorite is the one where she does the whole play on the pitchfork farmer and his wife painting we talked about in art class. Only I'm holding a vine-turning stick, and Beau is holding a watermelon. Sadly, it isn't ripe yet, but we're guessing the public won't know.

Beau may have griped and groaned through the whole thing, but he smiled when he was supposed to. I'm sure the thought of disappointing his momma was enough to keep him in line.

"I have what I need here. I'm just going to head back to the paper. I'd offer you a ride, but I'm on a tight deadline," Morgan says.

I shake her hand. "That's okay. I'm happy to wait here."

Beau already went to start checking the irrigation system.

The wind starts to pick up. Goosebumps spread across my arms. We were in such a hurry when we left that I forgot to grab my phone. There isn't really anything I can do to help Beau, so I head to the tailgate and have a seat. I let my legs swing, while I wait. Evening is my favorite time of the day. Normally, there would be the sound of chirping crickets, but the coming storm has sent them all into hiding. The wind picks up a little more, causing stray strands of hair to fly across my face. I don't mind, though. The rain hums in the distance, while I'm miles away, reflecting on today. Gramps always says that God has a perfect plan for us; we just have to listen.

A fat raindrop lands on my shoulder and makes its way down my arm.

"Beau, how much longer?" I ask.

At some point, he comes back to get some tools from the truck.

"Another five minutes," he calls back.

"Well, I just got hit by my first raindrop. You might want to hurry up."

"Bring me the wrench, will you?"

I grab it and hop off the tailgate. The rain drops are starting to fall more freely now. He finishes fixing the pipe, and we run back to the truck. I'm thankful I thought to switch to my boots. We make it back inside the truck just as the sky opens up.

"That was close," Beau says.

He turns the key in the ignition. It chugs, and then dies. He tries again. Nothing happens. On the third try, the engine finally comes to life. We both let out a breath. The dirt road is muddy and almost washed away in some areas. It makes the going slow. Luckily, Mr. Baron was smart enough to build large ditches on either side of the road. It protects the fields from taking on too much water.

We have about a half a mile to go when the pickup truck lurches.

"Was that because of the mud or the engine?" Either answer spells bad news.

"I think it was the engine," Beau says.

The truck sputters one last time, then dies.

We look at each other. The only sound is the thud of raindrops hitting the truck.

"Try to start it again." My voice raises at the end—partly in question, partly in demand.

Beau turns the key. Nothing.

"Try it again."

He does. Still nothing.

"If I do it again, I could flood the engine. Then we have bigger problems," Beau says.

"Okay, fine. What now?"

"Do you have your phone? I left mine at the office. I didn't want it ringing while on the news," he says.

"No." I point to my skirt. "No pockets."

Beau gives a slow nod like he's letting everything click into place.

"What do we do?" I ask, worry making me chew on my bottom lip.

"We can either wait it out or run it. Your call," he says.

"Did anyone know which field we were going to?"

"No. They knew we were headed out for pictures and that I was going to check irrigation, but there are a couple dozen places I could have checked. If we don't make it back soon, they'll start to worry."

"I guess we run it then." I see no other option at this point.

Beau starts rummaging through the back seat of the pickup truck.

"What are you doing?"

"Trying to find a jacket or long-sleeved shirt to put over our heads as we run," comes his muffled response.

After digging around, he pulls out an old work jacket and a flashlight.

"Halfway from here is an old lean-to shed. We'll stop there first. Wait, I'll come around to get you."

He clicks on the flashlight and throws the jacket over his head, jumping out the door. The rain is almost deafening. I watch the beam from the flashlight, so I can open the door as soon as he makes it around. I'm soaked before my feet even hit the ground. We run under the cover of the jacket, both of us slipping every now and again. The mud is thick and weighs me down, but I keep going. We don't talk; we just run. The rain is strong, and it stings as it pelts us running to the cover of the shed.

Breathing heavily, Beau asks, "Are you okay?"

"Yup, just wet," I get out, even with my teeth chattering.

"I think you should wear the jacket."

I don't argue. It hangs down to my knees, and I have to roll the sleeves up several times.

"Whose is this?"

"It's my old one."

"Thanks. If only the newspaper reporter could see me now."

"Or worse, what if this was another one of the channel 44 segments?" Beau asks. Then he imitates Stormy's voice, "And what do you think of your childhood friend now, Beau?"

I roll my eyes.

Back to his normal voice, dripping with sarcasm, he says, "Well, Stormy, she looks a lot more like a drowned rat than she used to and not quite as tall as she was this morning."

He points to my black and white polka dot boots, but now they're just brown, caked in brown mud.

"Okay," I scoff. "I think you're rested. It's time to run."

We make a mad dash the rest of the way. We come crashing into the office to find Mr. and Mrs. Baron, Bennett, and a few of the farm-hands in the process of creating a search party.

"Thank goodness," Mrs. Baron says. "We were about to send people out to look for you."

"The truck died for good this time, Dad," Beau informs him.

"But you two are okay?" Mr. Baron looks between Beau and me until we both nod.

"Bennett, call Grace's grandfather to let him know what happened and that they are fine now. You two, hot showers and tea. Now," Mrs. Baron orders, sounding more like a drill sergeant than a worried mom.

One of the really nice things about the office is that it's an old farmhouse. Mrs. Baron stocks it with just about everything because, like all southern girls, she likes to be prepared.

Warmed from the shower and in sweats, I drink my tea. Bennett sits at the table with me, while Mrs. Baron hums in the background. She's throwing something together for us to eat while we wait out the storm.

"Well, Watermelon Queen, was your first day all you expected it to be?" Bennett asks.

"Let's just say it was more than I planned for," I dryly reply.

Bennett laughs.

"This is going to be a fun year. I've always wanted a little sister, and now I have one," he says.

Bennett's comment about a little sister burns. Is that how he sees me? I've liked Bennett for so long. Not that I've ever let on to it, but I have been crushing. Hard. Being with the Barons so much and all the things Bennett says and does sucked me in and pulled me under his spell. I mean, a boy who's easy on the eyes and isn't afraid to work hard—how could I resist?

Beau pulls out a chair to the table, making it unnecessary for me to respond to Bennett.

"Well, baby brother, Grace won't tell me about this evening, so I guess it's up to you to tell us how it went," Bennett says.

"After the reporter took a million pictures, I had to fix the rusted irrigation pipe. I thought we'd be okay. I got us in the truck before the downpour, but the pickup died about a half a mile away from the house. Neither one of us had our cell phones. We knew you guys would be getting worried, so we ran for it. If Grace hadn't changed into her boots, I'm sure we'd still be running."

Mr. Baron walks into the kitchen.

"Enough talking for one night. You two are plain lucky the truck didn't quit any farther away," he says. "It's getting late, and the rain has died down a little. Bennett, take Grace home. Beau, you can follow them in the truck and bring Bennett back. Your mom and I will see you at the house."

The drive doesn't take long. Bennett parks my car as close to the porch as he can; then we both run for it. He heads for the headlights of the truck that Beau followed us in. I dart toward the porch. The light in the kitchen is on, indicating that Gramps is waiting up. I dart through the raindrops and hurry inside. I still have to talk with him about my day. It's kind of our thing—ever since the accident.

Chapter 4

THE WEEK AFTER THE PHOTO promotion flew by. I barely saw any of the Baron boys. They were working in the fields, and Mr. Baron was busy filling the orders that kept me at the desk in the office all day. So now, it seems odd that we are already in Texas.

Bennett pulls the last piece of luggage off the conveyer belt at the airport. He and Beau have been stacking it on a cart as best they can. Again, we look like we're staying for a month, instead of three days. We find our driver, holding a sign with *The Barons* printed in black formal script, among the men in black suits and sunglasses. Our driver opens the limo door and then works on getting our luggage into the trunk. I'm pretty sure it took some divine intervention to make it all fit, but the driver is successful.

The Southern Convention is in full swing when we make it down to the ballroom. We have a table waiting for us—just another one of the perks of being the incoming national president for the organization. Mr. Baron barely has time to sit down before several people converge on our table. All of them want to talk to him. *Schmooze him* is probably a better way to describe what they are trying to do. The queen coordinator from their organization comes over to collect me. She doesn't take much time to introduce herself.

"Let's walk and talk," she says.

We make a beeline for the stage. In the minute it takes to walk to the stage, I learn that I get to introduce myself to the general public and will be backstage with the girls before they go on the stage for the crowning moment.

I make quick work of my introduction, making sure to make the crowd laugh. I wave and chance a look at Mrs. Baron. She winks at me and smiles. I give a quick wave and head backstage to an entirely different atmosphere. Eight girls pace the room, trying to work out their nervous energy. Tonight, one of their lives will change. They'll get to do what I do—and am starting to love—be a spokesperson for the watermelon industry and travel the country.

"Hi, ladies," I greet them, trying to break the tension.

I get various responses—from smiles to outright being ignored. One girl is crying in the corner. She's beautiful with olive skin; long, black hair; and big, brown eyes; and she is touching up her makeup in the mirror.

"I'm not crying," she says.

"Okay."

"I think they put cilantro in the salsa. I'm allergic. It makes my eyes water like Niagara Falls."

"Can I help?" I offer.

She continues digging around in her makeup bag.

"Found it!" she says, pulling out what looks like a black marker. Then she starts lining her eyes with it.

"Are you lining your eyes with that?" I ask the obvious. I can't wrap my mind around it.

"Don't knock it 'til you try it," she says.

She looks over after she's done. I can't wipe the shocked look off my face fast enough for her not to see. She laughs and then says, "I like you. Don't worry—it's not my normal method. But I improvised."

The southern coordinator pokes her head in the room to call the girls to the stage. As they file past me, I wish them luck. Then, before the olive-skinned girl is out the door, she turns and tosses me her marker with a wink. I can't help but like her. She has spunk.

The Barons are waiting for me, and, thankfully, my dinner arrives soon after I take my seat. The business proceedings are a bit tedious, but I tune it out and enjoy my salmon. The boys are busy with their steaks and potatoes, so they don't have much to say either. By the time I'm finishing my tiramisu, the girls are on stage in their evening gowns. I have to hand it to marker girl. She glows on the stage. I glance sideways at the boys to see if they've been watching. Beau has his eyes on his dessert. Bennett is staring at marker girl with a weird look on his face.

The coordinator takes the stage and begins talking about the year the new queen is going to have. It's nothing I haven't heard before, so I lean over to Bennett and whisper.

"Are you okay?"

"Yeah. I just can't believe she's here," he says and nods toward marker girl.

"Who is she?"

"Noelle Stone," he whispers.

"So . . ."

"So, she goes to college with me. Same department. Different views on dirt."

"I see."

But I don't really. Who cares if people have different views on dirt? Who cares about dirt, anyway?

"And?" I whisper, trying to prompt him into explaining more.

"And nothing," he whispers back.

Bennett makes a face that indicates there's more to the story, but we don't have time to discuss it more.

"And the new Southern Watermelon Queen is Noelle Stone," the coordinator says into the mic.

Everyone stands and claps as Noelle takes center stage to receive her crown.

People crowd around Noelle as the queen coordinator tries to organize all of the photographs. Lightbulbs flash continuously. The Barons and I stand in line, waiting our turn.

"So, what has you so bothered about the new queen?" Beau asks Bennett.

"Who? Her?" Bennett points to Noelle. "I'm not bothered," he says.

"Right, that's why you keep folding and unfolding your arms," Beau says, skepticism heavy in his voice.

"Yeah, something's up. You looked weird when she came on stage." I needle him a little, trying to get a response out of him.

"You have a thing for her?" Beau asks.

"Yup, you guessed it. My brother, the genius," Bennett says. Sarcasm drips from his voice.

"Okay, man, just wondering what's up with you. Forget I asked." Beau puts his hands palm up in surrender.

Our turn with Noelle arrives. She turns to welcome us up, then stops. The smile on her face is frozen in place. Introductions are made. After all, Mr. Baron is the next national president. She can't afford to be rude to him.

"Bennett," she says, barely able to keep her dislike of him hidden.

"Ms. Stone," Bennett replies with a fake smile.

They stand there, staring at each other. The tension is so thick, I'm starting to get nervous. Who is this Noelle Stone that she can cause Bennett Baron, the ultimate gentleman, to lose his manners? I chance a look over at Beau. It's obvious by the grin on his face that Beau loves watching his brother squirm.

"Ah, you two know each other," Mrs. Baron says.

"Yes, ma'am. We go to school together and have the same major," Noelle says, her smile back in place.

"Great," Mrs. Baron says as she hooks an arm in Noelle's. "You'll have to tell me how my son is doing then."

"Mom, I don't think we should bother Noelle about me right now. She's got a line waiting for her," Bennett says.

"Nonsense, Bennett, your mother is charming. I'd love to chat with her," Noelle says, giving him a pointed look over her shoulder.

"Let's just get our picture with her and be done," Bennett says.

He starts arranging us as quickly as he can, barely waits for the flash of the photographer, and then ushers us all off the stage.

"Bennett Baron, what was that? You embarrassed me," Mrs. Baron says.

"Sorry, Mom, but that girl isn't as sweet-tempered as she'd have you to believe," Bennett says.

"I like her," I say.

This is a funny side of Bennett. I've never seen him ruffled like this before. And as terrible as it is, I can't stop myself from teasing him.

"Me, too," Beau says, getting in another jab at Bennett.

"You two would," he grumbles, crossing his arms.

"Either way, I'm the upcoming national president. You cannot be rude to people, even if you feel like it," Mr. Baron reprimands him in a hushed tone, not wanting anyone to hear the conversation.

Music starts to fill the room, stopping Mr. Baron's lecture. He offers his hand to Mrs. Baron and directs her to the dance floor. She looks over her shoulder and says, "I expect you to make it right, Bennett." Then she glides onto the dance floor. Bennett grunts in response and heads to the opposite side of the room from Noelle, leaving Beau and me standing there.

"I need a soda. You?" Beau asks.

"I'm okay. Thanks, though."

I make my way to one of the tables, where several people I know from our convention are seated. We talk business until a hand taps my shoulder. I look up to find a boy my age offering me his hand.

"Sorry to interrupt, but I was wondering if I could steal you away for a dance."

"I'd be glad to." I take his arm, and we head to the dance floor, making small talk.

"I'm Warren Hartley, by the way."

"Grace."

"So, Grace, what do you think of our convention so far?"

"It's nice. I like your new queen."

"That's funny. I was going to say the same thing about your organization's queen."

"Were you now?" I look away, trying to hide my blush.

"Yes, I've heard really great things about her. I wanted to see for myself."

"And what have you found so far?"

"She knows the business; she can dance; and she blushes."

I blush more, which only makes Warren laugh.

"So, tell me about you. It seems you have a pretty good read on me."

"Eighteen, the oldest son of the southern convention's president, watermelon farmer extraordinaire. At your service," he says with a smile.

The song comes to an end, so we head to the sectioned-off area that offers sofas for the guests to rest. He's cute in that boy-next-door way.

"I'll get us a couple of drinks. What'll you have?"

"A Shirley Temple."

He gives me a sideways grin, clearly making fun of my beverage choice.

"Hey, don't knock it until you've tried it." I smile big.

He nods his head and heads off to get us the drinks.

I scan the room. Mr. and Mrs. Baron are making the rounds, talking with everyone they see. Mr. Baron looks tired. It has to take a lot to run the farm and be the president for our organization. I see Bennett talking animatedly with the new queen, Noelle. By the looks of it, I don't think he's making his momma very proud right now. At least, he finally got around to apologizing. Noelle jabs her finger into his chest and then marches off. He heads off in the opposite direction and doesn't so much as look back. *Oil and vinegar*, I can't help but think.

"What are you doing?"

"Beau, what do you want?" I ask, irritated.

"Warren Hartley," he says.

"Yeah, what about him?"

"He's no good. You shouldn't be hanging out with him alone."

"Okay, thanks for the tip. Bye now." I wave my hand, trying to dismiss him.

"He has a reputation. Luke would not want you hanging out with him."

"No. You don't get to bring Luke into this. Where do you get off acting like you know what Luke would want?" I try to keep my voice neutral, but it comes out in a hiss.

"Just listen, would ya? Warren is a smooth talker with only one thing on his mind. It's a game to him."

I can see Warren making his way to the sofa.

"Thanks for the warning."

I turn and give him my back just as Warren makes it back. Both boys stand there, staring at each other, neither one wanting to budge. Finally, Warren says something.

"Baron."

"Hartley."

"Actually, Beau was just leaving." I cross my arms over my chest, while shooting daggers at him with my eyes.

"I was just coming over to let you know that my mom needs you for a minute, so I guess that means we're both leaving."

He points to Mrs. Baron, who is motioning for me to come join her.

I look over at Warren. "I'm sorry. I'll be back as soon as I can."

"No need to apologize. A queen's work is never done." He winks. "Save a dance for me."

"Happy to."

He hands me my drink and raises his own—a Shirley Temple like mine.

"I'll let you know what I think when I get that dance."

"C'mon, Grace, Mom's waiting." Beau offers me his arm, and I have no choice but to take it.

"Tell me you didn't buy that garbage," Beau drawls, sounding more annoyed than anything else.

"And if I did?"

"I'd say Luke was the smarter twin," he says, right before he delivers me to his mother.

I shove my reply back down my throat. Better not air Beau's and my dislike for one another to the national watermelon board.

"There you are, dear." Mrs. Baron begins making introductions around the group. We make polite conversation for the better part of an hour when Bennett taps on my shoulder.

"I haven't gotten to dance with our watermelon queen yet. If memory serves me right, I owe you a waltz. I guess this will have to do. May I have this dance?"

"You sure may, but be prepared to play twenty questions."

"Do I get to ask the questions or answer them?"

"Answer them. So, spill; what's the deal with you and the new Southern Watermelon Queen?"

"Nothing."

I'm not buying it.

"Try again."

"So, she and I go to the same school. We had this big project our entire class was working on. She had one idea about how to do it, and I had another. The professor said we had to work it out together."

"She sounds terrible." I gasp in mock horror. "Having to work to-gether? Well, I never."

"Har-dee-har-har. Aren't you funny?"

"It's one of my charms. But seriously, what was so bad about that?"

"Noelle wouldn't budge on her idea—no halfway ground at all."

"That would be difficult. I'm sorry I was teasing you."

"I'll forgive you, if . . . "

"If what?"

"You give me the next dance, too."

"Will do. That's easy peasy."

We fall silent and just dance. The song ends, and Bennett delivers me back to Mrs. Baron and the board. Before I can say thank you to Bennett, Beau is offering me his hand. It seems the Baron boys are determined to keep me away from Warren.

"I know what you're doing."

"Dancing?" Beau asks, being obnoxiously obtuse.

"Keeping me away from Warren."

"Now, why would I do that?"

"That's what I keep wondering."

"I owe it to Luke."

"Can you just stop?"

"Grace, I lost someone that day, too, you know. He was my best—"

"Just be quiet," I hiss because talking about Luke always reminds me of the accident. I can already feel the memories closing in.

Don't think about it, I tell myself when memories from the accident send tendrils of fear twirling down my spine. What I thought I'd bur-ied, resurfaces. The pain crashes around inside of me—suffocating me. Once in motion, it's hard to stop the onslaught of images flashing through my mind.

"You are so selfish," he accuses me. Anger flashes in his eyes, blaming me for everything.

"Selfish?"

I search desperately in the recesses of my mind for the off switch—anything to block out the pain and panic that claws its way up the back of my throat. It's a losing battle; the tears begin to pour out uncontrollably. I need to escape. Now.

"Excuse me. I need to go."

I break away from the dance floor and head to the bathroom. Thankfully, no one is in there. I reach the back stall and sit, not worrying at all about my evening gown. I hear the crush of the outer layers, but what do a few tattered pieces of fabric matter when he's just pushed my heart through a paper shredder?

Taking deep breaths, I pray from Psalms: *Lord, the Bible says You heal the brokenhearted and bind up their wounds. I need that right now. I need You. I hurt, Lord.*

Tears still stream down my face, but the suffocating pain recedes to a tolerable level. I fix my makeup in the mirror. Luckily, not too much damage was done. It will be dark in the ballroom, so no one will see my red-rimmed eyes. Before I leave the solitude of my bathroom sanctuary, I send up another prayer for strength and head back out to the ballroom to perform my duties as watermelon queen.

Chapter 5

I ROUND THE CORNER, WHERE Warren is leaning against the wall—one foot propped up behind him, his hands in his pockets.

"Are you okay?" he asks.

I look away, not really ready to talk about it with someone I met only an hour ago.

"You don't have to talk about it if you don't want."

"Thanks." I sigh, thankful that he understands.

Warren glances back into the ballroom.

"It looks like the convention will be in full swing for a while still."

"It's fine. I can manage."

"There's an ice cream shop just down the street. Want to go? My treat." He offers me his arm invitingly.

"I'd like that," I say, wrapping my arm around his. "Besides, I need a little mint chocolate chip therapy. It's a two-scoop kind of a night."

"Two scoops of mint chocolate chip?" Warren clutches his chest in mock surprise. "Why, Grace Summer, I do believe we may be soulmates. First, you introduce me to Shirley Temples, and now you have the same taste in ice cream. Stop. Wait. Let me get down on one knee. I need to ask you to marry me now."

I laugh, and then pull him along.

"Okay, Romeo, let's go get that ice cream you promised me."

We walk into the night air without much formality, other than when Warren holds the door for me and hands me my wrap. We walk a while in silence down a paved street in one of the older, more historic areas of Texas. The cobblestone streets and glass lamps add to the general magic of the night as stars glitter in the night sky. I can't take my eyes off of them.

"What's going on in that pretty head of yours?" Warren asks.

"I'm thinking about the stars."

"What about them?"

"I wish I had listened in science class when we were talking about them. Some are so bright, and others don't twinkle much at all. I wondered why."

"See that?" Warren says, pointing to one of the bigger stars in the sky. "That's part of the constellation Orion. The big star is a blue star."

"And what's so special about a blue star?"

"Nothing much, except it's three times the size of our sun."

"I'm impressed. I wouldn't have pegged you as a science guy."

"I'm full of surprises," he jokes.

"Interesting." I nod.

"First, you call me impressive, and now you add interesting. Keep it up, Grace, and I'll be in love before the night is through."

"Oh, stop it. Don't let your ego get too big. I'm sure you have flaws. I've just not found them out yet. Maybe you're a messy eater and, sorry, but that's a deal-breaker. Now, tell me what else you know about these blue stars."

He smirks a little.

"Not much more—only that they burn brighter and burn out faster than other stars. And an old wives' tale has it that if you see a blue star fall, then a miracle is headed your way."

We make it to the end of the street, where a Neapolitan-colored sign says *Homemade Sweet Treats*. Warren opens the door and ushers me inside. We find a booth by the window and dig into our ice cream.

"Warren?"

"Yes?" He waits for me to go on.

"I just wanted to say thanks is all."

"For what?"

"I don't know." I point to my ice cream. "I just needed this. And you. The conversation. I needed to forget for a while. You helped me do that."

"I'm happy to help, Grace. Any time you need a distraction, I'll be here—for mint chocolate chip ice cream or to talk about the stars."

"Why are you being so nice to me? I mean, you barely know me."

"True, but I'd like to get to know you a lot better. Besides, there's something about you I can't seem to shake."

"Is that a good thing?"

He raises my hand to his lips and gives a quick peck on the top of my hand.

"You tell me," he says.

"I'd say you haven't decided yet. And, well, neither have I."

The walk back is a quiet one—not awkward, just quiet. I can't stop thinking about the stars and what my miracle might be. We make it back to the hotel before I'm ready, heading straight back to the ballroom entrance.

"I'm not ready to go back in," I whine a little.

"Then we won't," he responds.

Warren and I stand in the entrance, just watching. Groups are still conversing, and couples sway on the dance floor. The Barons are chatting with various groups. It looks like my little trip went unnoticed. We are about to head in when an announcer takes to the mic and says, "Ladies and Gentlemen, it's that time of night. Let's welcome the queens to the dance floor to do the 'Watermelon Crawl.'"

I make my way to the center of the dance floor. It's only me and the Southern Watermelon Queen, Noelle. The music starts, and we start the line dance. Usually, there are more queens here, but, for whatever reason, this year, other organizations didn't send their girls. Everyone crowds around and watches the time-honored tradition.

Before too long, the voice on the mic is back, calling all past queens to join in the dance line. Mrs. Baron joins me, and several other ladies take to the floor, too. Mrs. Baron and I hook arms and do-si-do one last time before the entire dance floor is swarmed by convention-goers. Even Mr. Baron joins in. Not counting Warren, it's the most fun part of the evening and the last song of the night.

Everyone grabs their stuff from the banquet table and says their good nights. I see Noelle and head straight for her.

"I wanted to say congratulations one more time."

"Thanks," she says.

"So, I guess I'll see you next week at queen's training."

"I can't wait. We should sit together."

"I'd like that. We can get to know each other better. Don't worry—Bennett isn't coming." I can't resist saying it.

She pulls a face. "Good to know. Catch ya later."

We part ways, and I head toward the Barons. Mr. Baron is helping Mrs. Baron with her wrap, and the boys are lost in a conversation of their own.

"Grace, you were divine tonight," Mrs. Baron says.

"Thanks. I have to say, Mrs. Baron, you were great during the 'Watermelon Crawl.'"

I do a sassy, little cha-cha step. Mrs. Baron looks delighted and laughs a little. "Let's go to our rooms. We're all tired. And tomorrow, we have to be at the press conference pretty early."

With how busy we were, I had almost forgotten about being invited to join Noelle tomorrow for a ribbon-cutting ceremony for the new watermelon nursery. It houses thousands of tiny seedlings. Eventually, they'll be shipped all over the country to agricultural centers. We'll get a tour of the greenhouses and the packing plant before Noelle cuts the ribbon.

Mrs. Baron and I pull up to the curb and are greeted by the southern watermelon organization's president before we can both get out of the cab. Thanks to our morning coffee, I can respond with a smile. The publicity is good for the organization, which trickles down to the rest of the members in some shape or form. Noelle is already in the greenhouse, chatting with several of the agriculturists. News crews swarm around, setting up cameras and lights. The city's mayor is going to make a speech first. The new plant nursery has created several jobs in the community, so he wants to capitalize on the exposure.

We meet Linda, the news crew chief, and get our directions from her. It doesn't take long before we are in front of the cameras, smiling. Noelle cuts the ribbon to the applause of the crowd. A lady with a bright smile and green suit jacket with the nursery logo on it directs us toward a back door.

"I will be your guide today; I'm Helen, by the way. Follow me, please."

One of the news cameramen breaks off from the pack and follows us around as we walk down row after row of watermelon seedlings. They are labeled for different varieties, and some agriculturalists are taking dirt samples and plant readings as we pass by.

"Bennett would love this." I look over at Noelle, then wish I hadn't when I see her reaction. Trying to make it better, I add, "I bet you'd love to work on some of the samples yourself."

"It would be fun. Let's ask."

And before I know what's happening, we are in white lab coats and taking various samples of dirt. Noelle is in her element. She gets right to work. The cameraman pans all around us in an effort to get various angles.

"So, tell me more about this Bennett thing." I try to sound uninterested and use a spade to make little holes in the soil for the seedlings.

"Nothing to tell, really."

Noelle hands me one of the samples and points for me to put it in a certain carton. I do as she directs and say, "I saw him apologize to you at the convention last night. That's got to mean something right?"

"True, but it was a backhanded apology. He basically said he was sorry he was right and that I couldn't handle it."

"That doesn't sound like Bennett. He's usually so nice."

"Nice? I wouldn't put him in that category. I'd say he's more like a bee sting than anything else. You know, under your skin, annoying you, hurting you—"

"Okay, I get your point."

"He also said that the only reason I won my title is because my dad is the marketing board president."

"He didn't." I'm a little shocked that Bennett would hit that low.

"Truthfully, I'm sure it helped. But I am good at this, and I know all about the industry. I've been attending conventions since I was a little girl."

Noelle can come off as a know-it-all; but if Bennett said that, then honestly, I have no words left to defend him.

"Excuse me, ladies, but we need to get moving if we are going to get all of the footage we need," Helen says.

We take off our lab coats and continue the tour. After about another hour of walking and smiling, we are finished. There's no fanfare; the cameraman simply packs up his stuff and leaves. Mrs. Baron ushers me into the cab, and we make our way to the airport.

"That was a fun way to end this trip," Mrs. Baron says, looking happy.

"It was, wasn't it?"

She lets out a sigh. "Thank you, Grace."

"For what?"

"This," she waves her arms around the cab. "Doing the queen contest, being lovely and kind."

"You're welcome."

My voice rises a little in a question. I'm not sure what she expected me to say.

"Let's rest. We have an exhausting day. And it's not even lunch time yet."

I close my eyes and relax, thankful that the guys have all of the luggage waiting for us at the airport.

Chapter 6

ATLANTA AND THE QUEEN'S TRAINING seminar arrive without much ceremony. Unless arriving with the entire Baron family in tow counts. Mr. Baron and the boys have several meetings to attend about the national convention. Bennett is even speaking about soil pH or something like that. I stopped listening halfway through his overly animated discussion about dirt with the guys.

I'm not going to lie—having Warren in the picture gives me something better to think about than soil pH and a lot of other things, too. It's still tough being that person who hides her sadness with a smile. Everyone wants me to let it go. I just can't. What was the purpose in all of it? Is there a good reason for Luke's death? Because right now, I can't find one.

The boys head off to their meeting with a wave, leaving Mrs. Baron and me to ourselves.

"I know just what we need," she says.

"What's that?"

"Pedicures."

"That sounds amazing." I agree wholeheartedly. A little rest and relaxation never hurt anybody; besides, we have time. Especially since my training doesn't start until tomorrow. It will be a week of interview prep, information on what the watermelon has to offer nutritionally, practice in front of a camera, and photo shoots.

After we get our toes done, we have just enough time to make it to Bennett's presentation. We sneak in the back and find a few empty seats. Bennett is already at the podium. He's good. It's obvious that he has the respect of the audience. I chance a look around the room. I spot Noelle sitting by a pretty blonde. Probably another watermelon queen. I'm sure I'll meet her tomorrow. Bennett finishes his presentation to the applause of the crowd. He shakes a man's hand that has a striking resemblance to Noelle, then sits with Mr. Baron and Beau at their table. When the meeting is adjourned, we head straight for the guys, pleading hunger.

"So, where do you want to go?" asks Mr. Baron.

"There's this new sushi spot I heard about," Mrs. Baron offers.

The boys both collectively grunt.

"This is my last meal before I have to fly back to the farm. C'mon, Mom," Bennett jokingly whines.

"How about pasta?" I suggest.

"Better than raw fish," Beau says.

"I'll ask Scott Stone. He's here a lot. He'll know a good place," Mr. Baron says.

I lean over to Bennett. "I take it that's Noelle's father."

"You guessed it, little sister."

"Sorry, big brother." The words flow out easier than I thought they would. I don't even trip over them. Maybe, deep down, I always knew we were more like siblings than anything else.

"Fix your face," I whisper.

Bennett looks at me weird.

"You look like you just ate the watermelon rind. I'm assuming it's because Mr. Scott makes you think of Noelle."

Bennett's reply is cut off because Mr. Scott and Noelle join our group, so Mr. Baron shakes hands with him and handles the introductions.

"We were wondering if there are any great pasta places around here," Mrs. Baron asks.

"Noelle would know. What's the name of the place you and your mother always go to?"

"The Pasta Bowl," Noelle says.

"Yes, that's it. You guys should go there."

"Thanks. We will. You two care to join us?" Mr. Baron asks.

"I can't. We have a big meeting tomorrow about a new initiative for the industry. I need to go over the presentation notes. I can't tell you more than that. But Noelle can go."

Mr. Stone is the president of the watermelon marketing board. The board's main goal is to create awareness about the watermelon and show people how versatile a fruit it is.

"That's okay, Dad. I'll just order room service."

"We insist," Mrs. Baron says. "You and Grace get along so well, and you should get out while you can. This week will be a busy one."

With no way out, Noelle says, "Thank you, ma'am. I'll get my coat."

Mr. Baron and Mr. Stone talk a little bit more about the week and what's in store for everyone before we head to the front of the hotel. Bennett gives the valet our ticket stub and tries not to sulk. I can't help but snicker a little.

"What's so funny?" Beau asks.

"Bennett. Noelle really gets under his skin."

"Yeah, he's into her. He just won't admit it."

Not willing to let it go, I prod Beau for more. "Why?"

"Because she challenges him and doesn't go all stupid around him like most girls."

The Tahoe pulls up, and we all climb in. I wouldn't have thought about it that way. Noelle is one of the first girls that hasn't gone all googly eyes once she's seen Bennett. He's not used to someone not finding him charming. Noelle will do him some good if for no other reason than to show him people can be immune to his southern charms.

The Pasta Bowl has chairs set up at little round tables with cream-colored tablecloths. On the tables, burgundy candles glow softly. Grape vines hang down the trellises. It gives a very Tuscan feel to the atmosphere.

"What a romantic little place, Noelle," Mrs. Baron says as Mr. Baron offers his arm to her.

We follow the hostess to a back table on the veranda. Twinkling lights hang from the ceiling, and violin music floats through the air. We take our seats, but Mrs. Baron waits to sit down.

"Noelle, will you switch seats with me, so I can sit by John—seeing how he's flying out tonight, too?"

"Of course," Noelle says.

This lands her directly next to Bennett. If I didn't know any better I would say Mrs. Baron was playing matchmaker with those two. A look from Beau tells me he's on the same page as I am. Well, the good news is she will have less time to focus on me and Beau. Before my mom died, Mrs. Baron had this crazy notion that she and Mom could be more than just sisters in friendship by marrying me and Beau off together. Beau and I have been the target of many of her matchmaking schemes. For once, I get to sit back and enjoy the show.

The food is amazing—by far the best breadsticks I have ever had in my life. Mrs. Baron tells funny stories from her time as the watermelon queen. Bennett and Noelle tolerate each other's presence, and Beau and I get a break from Mrs. Baron's meddling ways. For me it's a win, win. We top the night off with cannoli drizzled with chocolate sauce and talk about Mr. Baron and Bennett's red-eye flight home.

On the way to the airport, the conversation changes to tomorrow's meeting for Noelle and me and the photo shoot we will be doing.

"I've heard we'll be on the boardwalk with bicycles," Noelle says.

She has an inside edge, since her father is on the promotion board and in charge of organizing a lot of these events.

"Did your dad say how they would put the watermelon in the shoot?" I ask.

"No. We weren't really talking about it. I heard him on the phone."

We pull up to the curb and drop Mr. Baron and Bennett off. They have a long night ahead of them and then work in the fields in the morning. Mr. Baron gives Mrs. Baron a kiss goodbye, and they head into the airport. Mrs. Baron pulls away from the curb and starts talking about outfits for tomorrow's meeting.

"Let's put you in that emerald green jumpsuit tomorrow and the gold bangle bracelets."

"Yes, ma'am."

"Did you bring your wedges? They will be the most comfortable with the day they have planned for you."

"Yes, ma'am," I answer again.

Mrs. Baron smiles at my response, then takes a phone call.

"So, I'm assuming your dad and mom sponsored you?" I ask Noelle.

"Yeah, they did. I've wanted to be a watermelon queen from the time I was old enough to travel with Mom and Dad on business trips."

"Cool."

"Yeah, so how do you know the Barons?"

I swallow the sandy glob that always seems to form when questions get too close to Luke and my mom and dad.

"My mom and Mrs. Baron were best friends. Plus, my brother and I used to play with Beau. Luke and he were best friends. I would tag along."

"Were?"

"Car accident," is all I can get out before I have to look out the window, unable to look Noelle in the eyes any longer.

"Oh, sorry. I shouldn't have asked."

"It's okay."

Little by little, I can feel the waves of sadness start lapping at me. I let out a breath, trying to push the pain back down into the tiny hole in my chest where I keep the pain.

"So, I'm an idiot," Noelle says. "Let's change the subject. How about boys?"

She crosses her eyes. "I'll go first. Ask me what you want to know."

It's a distraction, but I'll take it.

"It's more of a statement," I warn. "Bennett Baron."

"Ugh, you would."

"And . . ."

"And he's annoying—cute—but too annoying for words."

"Interesting," I open my eyes wide, teasing her.

"Anyway, how about you? Any boys I should know about?"

"Warren Hartley. I met him at your convention, actually."

"Be careful."

"Why?"

"Warren hasn't ever really done anything, but he seems to enjoy the game—if you know what I mean."

"You sound like Beau."

"Ah, Beau doesn't like him either? Well, we both know why."

"Yeah, he's appointed himself as my watchdog. Says my brother, Luke, would have wanted him to."

"That's the line he's trying to feed you. Did it work?"

"What's that supposed to mean?"

"Oh, you'll figure it out."

The Tahoe pulls up to the front of the hotel, and Mrs. Baron gives the valet our key. Noelle and I part ways with a promise to sit with each other tomorrow.

Chapter 7

IT LOOKS LIKE I'M THE last one to arrive. Mrs. Baron dropped me off at the door but didn't walk me in. This is one of those rare times when the queens are left without their sponsors. We are all meeting each other for the first time, so the thought is it will be more relaxed without them. My guess is that the marketing board wants to be able to get through everything they have to show us without a hundred interruptions from our sponsor families.

The meeting room is smaller than I had imagined, especially because all eyes are trained on me as I enter the room. Noelle was true to her word and saved a spot for me. The national queen sits beside her. They come from the same watermelon organization. I take my seat by Noelle, and she does the introductions.

"Grace, meet Becca Spellman. Becca, this is Grace Summer, the Midwest Watermelon Queen."

"Hi," I greet her, smiling wide.

"Hey, so Noelle has told me all about you."

"All good things, I hope."

She laughs and nods her head yes.

"Ladies, if I could have your attention, we will go ahead and start the meeting," Noelle's father says.

We all sit up a little straighter and face the front of the room.

"My name is Scott Stone. I'm the president of the watermelon marketing board, and we are happy to have you with us today. Let's start by everyone introducing themselves."

The marketing board members stand up and give a brief rundown of what they do for the organization and what they will be teaching us today. Next, we take turns telling about ourselves.

Noelle goes first and tells a funny story about her dad, which really breaks the ice a bit. She's a natural at this, which is good. Some people would accuse her of winning the title purely because of who her father is.

Then, we have Audrey Davis, the Southwest Watermelon Queen. Blonde and blue-eyed, she seems to be able to turn anything she touches to gold. She's got a laundry list of accomplishments.

The Northeast Queen is Rosanne Jackson. She wears her hair in a brown bob and seems to like flipping it. I stop listening to what she says and count the number of flips instead. Grand total for three minutes of talking is twenty-three.

Victoria Marsh is a college student at Oregon Coast Community College. She seems cool. She goes by "V" and loves to paddleboard. She lives in her own little 1947 Ruby Red Shasta RV with her dog, Peachy. She's beautiful, with long, wavy, chestnut hair. She has a very laidback air about her, which will be nice for a change.

I go next. I leave out the sad stuff, but I tell them about growing up with Beau and Bennett. I talk about what I play on the radio of the tractor to drive the boys nuts, which gets me a laugh. I sit down to applause, pleased with how my introduction went.

Lastly, Becca stands up and talks about her year so far and how excited she is to be here. She reminds us that next year, it will be one of us getting a second year of fun. We all clap one more time until Mr. Stone takes the podium again to introduce Anne. Her job for today is to make sure we all know how to choose a ripe watermelon and to make sure we understand the health benefits. She points out that when we do the Fresh Tour road trip—or Fresh for short—we will have to help the consumer pick out a ripe melon at all the different grocery stores we go to.

We spend the better part of two hours learning about the nutritional selling points of the watermelon before she calls it to a halt. She gives us a fifteen-minute break, so they can set up for Chef Michael, who will be teaching us watermelon carving tips. Chef Michael is well known for his skill. He's been on multiple TV shows, including *Good Morning America*.

We all gather around the snack table, while we wait.

"I can't wait for the photo shoot later today," Audrey pipes up.

"Yeah, I've heard they are using retro bikes," Rosanne joins in.

The word retro is all V needs to get started.

"I love retro things. My RV is my prized possession. I'm still in the process of remodeling it, but I love the process of making it my own."

"Is it lonely?" Becca asks.

"Not really. My brother's in the Marines, and Mom lives in a tiny apartment. My dog, Peachy, and I visit her a lot."

Anne drops by the snack table and grabs a plate of watermelon salsa and hummus.

"We're starting in one minute, ladies."

Chef Michael takes the stage and begins demonstrating various ways to carve the watermelon. He's high energy, but I zone out. We never really have to carve our own watermelons. The marketing board makes sure that someone else does that. It wouldn't do any good if a queen butchered the watermelon display—or her hand, for that matter.

Chef Michael is on his fifth carving when I finish my coffee. I'll give him this—he's fast. He finishes with flair, and we all clap for him because the watermelon looks amazing. He's done a hummingbird drinking nectar from a flower on the outside of the rind.

Anne takes the stage again.

"Okay, girls, it's time for the photo shoot. Follow me, and I'll get you to your trailers for hair and makeup."

We follow her like sheep, not knowing where we are going.

"I hope they feed us. The snacks from earlier weren't really enough to fill me up." Becca rubs her stomach.

"I'm hungry, too," I agree.

Anne stops by the first set of trailers and calls us out by our titles. Noelle, Audrey, and Rosanne take the first three. We follow Anne a little further down. People are working on decorating the set. Flowers and watermelon vines are being brought in by the dozens. Large lights are being set up around the perimeter. The last three trailers come into view. Anne points us each in the direction we are to go. Nervous anticipation charges through my stomach and down my legs as I open the door. I am in no way prepared for the lady with spikey red hair standing on the other side.

"Hi. I'm Maggie, your hair and makeup artist."

"Grace." I point to myself.

"I know. I was assigned to you last week. We had to submit hair and makeup ideas prior to today."

"Cool. So, what do you need from me?"

"Nothing. Take a seat, and relax." She spins the chair around, waiting.

I'm practically blinded by the lights when I swivel around to face the mirror. "So, what's the plan?"

"Natural beauty is what we're going for."

She starts by contouring my face. Then she adds a layer of foundation.

"Don't worry; it will photograph perfectly," she promises in response to the worried look on my face.

"You're the expert." I try to sound reassured.

She finishes with my eye makeup and then comes at me with what looks like spiders.

"Uh, what are those?"

She laughs a little. "False eyelashes."

"Did you just put glue on those things?"

Blowing on the white, gloopy dots she'd placed along the edge, she says, "Yup. Don't worry; they'll come off with soap and water."

"If you say so." Doubt creeps into my voice.

She twirls me away from the mirror and has me lean back in the chair, while she comes at me with those spidery false eye lashes.

"Relax, and close your eyes," she says.

When she's done, they aren't as bad as I had expected. It takes a minute or two of fluttering my lashes to get used to them, but I do easily enough. She adds lipstick to the mix, then moves on to my hair.

"We're doing soft waves." She takes the curling wand to my hair. She pulls pieces back in the front and lets other tendrils fall down the sides and back. I watch in the mirror, mesmerized as she turns me into a summer beauty.

"All done." She puts her hands on her hips and steps back to admire her handy work.

"Wow. You're amazing. I love it. Thanks!"

"You're welcome."

The door to the trailer opens.

"Hi, ladies. I have lunch."

It's Warren. He's loaded down with sandwiches and fruit.

"Grace, you look beautiful, but, then again, you always do," Warren says.

"Thanks. What brought you here?"

He raises the sandwiches. "Lunch."

The smell of the sandwiches makes my stomach rumble, reminding me just how long ago breakfast was.

"Dad donated the watermelons for the shoot. He couldn't leave the farm, so he sent me," he explains.

"Lucky for me." I smile up at him. Then, before he can say anything else, I ask, "So, what did you bring for lunch? I'm starving."

We sit at the table in the trailer and eat. Maggie stays with us, telling stories of her previous clients. Warren—ever the gentleman—takes our trash and throws it away for us. He looks at his watch, then back to me.

"The photo shoot is scheduled to start soon. They were talking about the start time when I dropped off the melons," he says, offering me his arm. "Grace, you should probably already be at the clothing trailer. I'd be happy to walk you there."

He bows a little, still offering his arm, and I take it. We head down through the warehouse toward the clothing trailer.

"I'll see you at the shoot." Warren leaves me at the door.

"Looking forward to it," I say, before going inside.

Several girls are already dressed but are getting finishing touches done to the clothes. Noelle is standing there with her arms straight out in front of her, while someone works on taking in the sides of her shirt. Audrey is being given a different shirt to try on, while the rest of the girls sit in chairs along the perimeter of the area. V has on two different shoes as two people talk over the merits of each one and which pair will go best with the color scheme. I head over to Anne, who seems to be directing the entire event, and get the clothes with my name on them.

"Put these on. Then get in line behind Noelle to have any alterations done."

I take my peach-colored skinny jeans, white tank top, and faded blue jean shirt and head to the dressing room. The pants fit everywhere but in the waist. The white tank top is a little big; but, other than that, everything seems to work well. Or so I thought. When the seamstress gets a look at me, she starts rolling up the sleeves of the jean shirt. Then she pulls the tank top in on the sides and safety pins the sides, so the tank is more figure-fitting. She starts taking in the waist of my pants while I'm still in them and ties off the thread before the thought even registers that she's basically sewing me into them. With a quick twist, she takes the edges of the jean shirt and ties them in a knot in the front. She does one quick walk around.

"Done." She throws up her arms like they do on *Cake Wars* when the time is up.

We congregate at the door and head to the shoot. Everyone is dressed in varying shades of pastels. The color scheme is very light and frothy. Warren is placing some of the extra watermelons toward the side of the shoot. I give him a wave, and he winks back in return.

The set has robin's-egg-blue bikes with baskets attached to them. In the basket are watermelons and vines hanging down some of them, while others have bright red slices of watermelon and sunflowers. We each take a bike and stand there. They move our hands or our faces every so often. Then the fans start up, and our hair looks like it's blowing in the wind. Someone turns on the music, and the photographer starts clicking away. He moves all around us, giving directions when needed.

"Move your bike handle here." Then he shouts, "Look to your right—no, your other right. Act like someone said something funny."

The photographer calls for a break. They start removing the bikes from the shoot and bring in other products that we need to showcase—some of the melons Chef Michael carved, watermelon popsicles, beautiful watermelon dishes, and watermelon merchandise. The ad campaign plans to place different advertisements in some of the more commercial magazines. They are also doing a six-page spread in *Growing Vines Magazine*, a hip, new magazine that has to do with healthy living and eating. One of the photos taken today will go on the front cover.

I make my way over to Warren.

"So, what do you think?"

"I think you look pretty."

"We've established that, you goof. But, thank you. I was talking about the photo shoot."

"I was in on last year's shoot, and I'd say this one tops it by far. The marketing board really stepped up their game."

"Good." I clap my hands, excited.

Warren laughs. "You're so cute," he says, putting his hands on my shoulders.

They call us back to the shoot before too long.

"I gotta go." I'm a little disappointed. Spending time with Warren always puts me in a good mood.

"I'll be here when you're done. Maybe we can grab a bite for supper."

"Sure. Good idea. We can talk about it when I'm done."

For this section, the photographer takes singles of each of us with various watermelon products. We get to show a bit more individuality, which is fun.

Noelle gets the watermelon carvings from Chef Michael. She puts on a chef's hat and holds some of the carving tools. She looks very comfortable in front of the camera. Her dark hair and eyes shine. Then, the photographer pulls a few more of us in. We eat watermelon in the background.

I'm up next. He gives me a checkered yellow towel and a slice of watermelon. I turn to the side and hang the towel over my shoulder. They place the watermelon in front of me. The photographer snaps away. He moves around me and gets pictures from every angle. Then, I turn to the front and hold the watermelon out in front of me as far as I can. I hear the snaps of the camera shutter opening and closing.

The cameraman snaps his last shot and sends me on my way. Warren is waiting for me at the edge of the set, so I head in his direction. I hear the camera begin snapping again as the cameraman starts working on the next girl's shoot.

"Care to take a walk with me?" Warren asks.

"Yes, please."

We have a good hour before the individual shoots will be done, and we have to report back for the final meeting today.

"So, tell me, what does the son of a large watermelon farmer do all week?"

"Well, I travel for Dad a lot. Being eighteen and able to take online classes helps. My teachers are willing to work around my schedule for me."

"That's lucky. How do you turn assignments or projects in?"

"The program is designed for students like me. I watch class lectures online when I have time on the plane or in the car."

"Do you ever feel like you're missing out?"

"Okay, Dr. Phil . . . No, not really. I get to travel and basically get to hang out with pretty girls like you."

"Girls? Like the plural form?"

"Yes—*girls*. I see them all the time, silly, but I only want to spend time with one of them in particular."

"Very smooth." Relief washes over me that he's not just stringing me along.

"I thought so." He winks, and we continue walking.

The last session of the day is a little awkward. It's the "How to Get Rid of a Customer Who is a Little Too Flirty or Inappropriate" session. We watch a video about it and then role-play with one another. V and I are paired together, and we can't stop giggling. V is playing a seventy-year-old man who "just can't walk away from a pretty girl." She uses a crotchety, old voice, wobbling her lines, so we crack up again. Anne walks by, clearing her voice and giving us a look. We wipe the smirks off our faces and try to take it more seriously.

"So, what's the deal with you and Warren?"

"Cute, isn't he?"

"You can't answer a question with a question. It's rude."

"I just did." I can tell V wants more, so I go on. "But, really, there's not too much to say. There's definitely a spark, but we live in different states. So, there's that."

"Yeah, but they're mega rich, and it's not like Warren couldn't travel to you any time he wanted."

"True. We will just have to see what happens—and if I get Beau to leave me alone long enough to see where this thing with Warren is going."

"He does guard you pretty closely. Know why that is?"

Not wanting to bring up the accident, I play it down. "It's a long story. Not important really."

Finally, Anne calls a halt to the day, so we pack up for our hotel rooms. I walk straight to Warren, so I'm saved from any more prying questions from V. He grabs my bag and offers me his arm.

"Walk you to your ride?"

"Of course." I take his arm, unable keep the grin off my face.

"Can you do dinner tonight?" he asks.

"That would be great."

"So, I'll pick you up around seven tonight."

"I'll be ready."

We round the corner to find Beau waiting for us, with his typical frown in place.

"Where's Mrs. Baron?" I ask, annoyed to see Beau there.

"The airport."

"What?"

"She's okay. It's Dad. He fell and broke his leg pretty badly. Mom is flying home to see about that. She'll be back tomorrow some time."

"So, what are we supposed to do?"

"Head back to the hotel and wait for an update. No going out."

"It looks like we are staying in tonight." I look up at Warren. I want to be there when we hear about Mr. Baron anyway.

"Warren, want to join us for a pizza?"

"Sorry. Not happening," Beau says.

I cross my arms and give him the death glare.

"Mom's orders, not mine."

"It's fine, Grace," Warren says. "I'll catch up with you tomorrow."

He walks us to the Tahoe and opens my door, while Beau gets in the driver seat.

"Let me know what you find out about Mr. Barron."

"You'll be the first to know."

"Until tomorrow, pretty girl," he says, shutting the door.

Chapter 8

"SO, WHAT HAPPENED EXACTLY WITH your dad?"

"All I know is that the wagons were coming in, and Dad was organizing them by the packing shed. Bennett said something about a wagon coming loose and Dad jumping out of the way as best he could."

"It's only a broken leg. Right?"

Beau turns into the hotel entrance and parks the car for the valet.

"Yes. He's banged up, but the biggest issue is a broken leg and a minor concussion."

We step out of the car, and I grab our stuff from the back seat, while Beau talks with the valet. We don't resume our conversation until we are back in our rooms.

"So, what's that mean for the farm?"

"Bennett will run the operation. I'm assuming Mom will be back tomorrow. We'll get more from her when she calls us tonight."

"Beau?"

"Yeah?"

"I'm sorry about your dad. I'm worried about him, too."

"Thanks."

We face one another in the living area of the suite, neither one of us knowing what to say or do to make the situation any better. All of this makes me miss home.

Finally, Beau breaks the silence. "I'm hungry. How about you?"

"I could eat. Do you care to order a pizza?"

"I can do that."

"I'm going to call Gramps for a bit."

"Sure. The usual?"

"Perfect. Thanks."

The phone rings three times before Gramps answers it.

"Hi, Gramps."

"Hi, Short Stack."

"Did you hear about Mr. Baron?"

"I did. Sounds like a freak accident to me. He's lucky. That's for sure."

"Yeah, so I'm assuming Mrs. Baron is at the hospital with him."

"Yes, she's home. I picked her up from the airport. Bennett has been in the fields all day, trying to stay on top of things."

"That's good."

"I talked with Bennett. It sounds like the recovery will take some time."

"That's what Beau and I were afraid of."

"It will all work out. It always does."

I catch him up on my day and the game plan for the next one. We hang up when Beau hollers that the pizza's here. I quickly throw my hair up in a topknot and change into leggings and a sweatshirt. I'm too hungry to take the time to do anything more. It looks like Beau had the same idea. He's in sweats and a faded t-shirt. He's got the pizza box open on the coffee table and the first slice in his mouth. I plop down on the other end of the sofa and unceremoniously dig in. "This almost feels like old times." I sigh a little, remembering what we used to be like when Luke was still here.

Beau gives me a sideways glace and pulls the cheese back into place on his pizza. Then, he clears his throat. "Grace?"

"Yeah?"

"I want to ask you something about that night. I know it's still pretty raw for you."

Something about the nostalgia of tonight makes me stronger, almost like I need to talk about it, too. "It's okay. I think I can manage."

"Luke and I had fought that day. Did he mention anything in the car about it?"

"I can honestly say the fight must have been over in his mind, and you were forgiven. He was talking about meeting up with you the next day."

Relief washes over Beau's face. "Baseball. We were going to hit the batting cages. Dad had given us the day off for whatever reason."

I rub my hands over my temples, then down my face.

"What are you thinking about?" he asks.

"That day."

"Can you tell me?"

"We were in the car; Dad was singing off-key to the radio. Mom was laughing at him because she knew he did it on purpose. Luke and I were in the back seat, complaining about the cramped leg room in our compact car, like we always did, just to get Dad to stop singing and give his usual "money doesn't grow on trees" speech. Luke and I would take turns seeing how many times a day we could get him to give it. I think he was on to us, but he gave us what we wanted and started giving his normal speech."

I pause for a breath. I really don't want to cry in front of Beau.

"Are you okay? Do you want to stop talking about it?" he asks.

I shake my head and go on.

"Dad stopped at the four-way and then took off. We heard the horn before we saw the semi. All I remember is Luke unbuckling his seat belt and throwing himself over me to protect me. You know the rest. Mom and Dad were dead on impact."

I feel lighter somehow. It's the first time I've told the story since the police officer took the original statement. But I still can't finish the story, so Beau picks up where I left off.

"Luke died at the scene," he whispers.

A couple tears leak out of the corner of my eye. I wipe them away quickly before Beau can see.

Trying to change the subject a little, I ask, "What did you two fight about that day, anyway?"

Beau stares at me with a weird look on his face but doesn't give me an answer.

"You wouldn't believe me if I told you."

"Well, I just answered your questions. Can't you answer mine?"

The phone rings, bringing us back to the present, and we immediately wonder about Mr. Baron. Beau answers it quickly. He begins pacing around the room, grunting in response every so often. When he finally hangs up, I'm worried.

"Well?" I prompt him, unable to wait any longer.

"Dad needs surgery. Six weeks minimum recovery. Mom's not leaving him at the hospital."

"Oh no. Is he taking it very well?"

"It's Dad. What do you think?"

Mr. Baron is probably miserable. And while the pain may be bad, what really would be bothering him is the fact that he's down during watermelon season.

"Poor Mr. Baron." And then it hits me. "Uh, what about us?"

"One-and-a-half days. Do you think we can make it without driving each other insane?"

I roll my eyes in response.

"I guess it's just you and me, kid," Beau says, reverting to his favorite childhood nickname for me.

"Beau, you are five months older than me. I don't think 'kid' is really that accurate."

Tonight was nice. We hit some kind of truce. Talking about the accident wasn't fun, but it helped.

"Thanks for the pizza and conversation," I say, heading toward my room.

"No problem. See you in the morning."

I close my door and crawl into bed. I send Warren a text about Mr. Baron and shut my light off. Tomorrow will be here in about six hours, and Mrs. Baron won't be here to help.

Most of the time, mornings are my favorite part of the day, but this one is on the other side of just a few hours of sleep. *Ugh.* I throw the fourth outfit on the bed, hopping across the room with only one high heel on. Beau knocks on the door.

"Grace, are you okay in there? I've heard you mumbling in there for the better part of twenty minutes."

"I'm fine," I shout through the door, when, really, I'm anything but. I can't figure out what to wear. We are doing the interview and television portion today. I give up and put on what I would wear—black leggings and a red tunic. I pull my hair up in a bun and slap on some red lipstick. I slide on my black Converse and add diamond earrings. It looks like I've headed into the main room just in time. Black smoke is coming out of the toaster. Beau just keeps pushing buttons on it.

"Doing okay over there?" I ask, sliding onto a bar stool.

"No, this is the third piece I've burned."

I can't help it. I laugh.

"Here, let me help you. Who would have thought that it only takes a toaster to defeat you?"

"Yeah, yeah, but you're right, my ego can't take it. Let's go get coffee at the corner bakery. My treat."

I grab my bag and jacket. Beau calls the valet as we quickly walk to the corner bakery. The line is short, and we make it back to the hotel just as the Tahoe pulls up to the curb. It's a comfortable silence in the car. Beau focuses on driving, while I text Warren back.

Before long, we pull up, and Beau parks the car on the curb.

"I'll be here to get you at noon. Mom emailed me the schedule. I know you should be done by then."

"That's ok. Warren's picking me up."

"No, he's not," Beau says.

"'Fraid so," I shoot back, opening the door.

Beau grabs my arm.

"Grace, I said no."

"And I say you are not the boss of me, Beau Baron. Warren and I have a date."

I get out of the car and force myself not to slam it shut. It's not the door's fault that Beau is so pig-headed.

"I'll be here when you're done today," he warns.

"You do that." My voice is laced with frustration.

Obviously, our short-lived truce is over.

Chapter 9

WE SETTLE BACK INTO A routine on the farm. Mr. Baron grudgingly does the office work, while the boys work in the fields. I've been put to work in the packing shed with Mrs. Baron. Raul, one of the farmhands, pulls up the wagon trailers, and we move the melons to the conveyor belt that will wash and dry them. The melons roll out onto another conveyor belt, and we sort them based on quality. Ones go to supermarkets and other distribution centers. Twos will go to the farmer's markets or be sold from the produce stand here.

It's an important job. If someone hasn't been trained to spot what makes a melon a two, they could let too many pass. It would be just as bad if they graded the melons too hard and didn't allow them to make it on the semi-truck. That's why Mrs. Baron and I do the sorting. Then, we hand them off to workers, who will put them in bins after another worker puts the stickers on the melons. It's a grueling process; but miss one step, and we have to start all over—which, luckily for me, means Mrs. Baron can't talk much. Bennett brings in the next three wagons, all attached to one another, and we start the whole process over. When the last pallet is loaded onto the semi, we break for lunch.

The Baron boys are waiting by the truck. We all slide in and head to the office.

"How are the vines?" Mrs. Baron asks the boys.

"Good. We'll still get several more rounds off of the southern fields," Beau says.

"The fields by the pond need to be sprayed again. I'll talk with Dad about it at lunch," Bennett says.

Bennett pulls up to the office and drops us off before pulling around to the back of the house. Mr. Baron is sitting behind the desk, working on the load orders.

"How's it going?" I ask.

"Okay," he grumbles.

"The boys have it under control." I go on when I see Mr. Baron's look. "But they do want to talk to you about a few things at lunch."

I offer to help him to the table, but he shoos me away, grabbing his crutches.

Mrs. Baron puts chicken salad sandwiches, watermelon slices, and potato chips on the table as the boys sit down. Mr. Baron blesses the food, and we all dig in.

"Well, boys, what do you have to report?" Mr. Baron asks.

"The southern fields are producing really well. We may get two more rounds out of them. Some of the northern fields are almost done producing. We may have to send a few workers out in a day or two to see if we missed any, but I'd say we're done there," Beau says.

"Good, good. How many twos are we getting?"

"Not many." At least I'm able to give him good news. "The crop is solid."

Mr. Baron nods.

"Dad," Bennett says, "the fields by the pond need to be fertilized badly. Some weed killer would be good, too."

"How far behind are they?" Mr. Baron asks.

"We can catch them up if we get them sprayed by the end of this week."

My phone buzzes with a message from Warren.

Miss you.

I type back. *Miss you, too.*

MAP is coming up. Can't wait to see you.

I've been secretly counting down until we can head to New Orleans and the Marketing and Advertising of Produce Convention—or MAP, for short. But before I can respond to him, Mrs. Baron asks me a question. Sighing, I put the phone away.

"Grace, tomorrow you have the *Lifestyle* show on Channel 44 and a couple of radio spots. Are you ready?"

"Yes, I am. What do you want me to wear?"

"You'll have your crown on. I was thinking the green, button-up dress and the watermelon bangle."

"Sounds good."

I couldn't really care less, but it matters to Mrs. Baron what I wear, so I let her worry about it.

The TV station studio is set up with lights and cameras. The lifestyle section has a small leather sofa and a coffee table. The production chief directs Mrs. Baron and me to the set and gives us a quick rundown of the schedule.

"We will do a five-minute Q and A here and then head over to the table for you to do your watermelon carving."

"Perfect. Can I go ahead and set out my carving utensils and prep the melons?"

"Good idea. You'll be on in about twenty minutes."

"What are you going to make, Grace?" Mrs. Baron asks.

"A panda. It's not too hard, and I can make it in the allotted time frame of the segment," I answer, and Mrs. Baron nods her head in agreement.

We organize everything and cut down some of the watermelons, so those parts will already be completed for the taping.

Mrs. Baron smiles her approval just as Stormy Meryweather walks in and directs me to take my seat. Several camera crew members take their spot for the broadcast. The production chief counts down from three with his fingers, then points to Stormy.

"Good morning. Stormy Meryweather here with special guest, Grace Summer, the Midwest Watermelon Queen." She turns to look at me and says, "Grace, welcome. We're glad you're here with us."

"Thanks. I'm happy to be here," I reply in my best TV voice.

"So, tell us, what have you been up to since the last time we chatted during your homecoming event?"

"I've been lucky enough to travel to Texas to the Southern Watermelon Convention and get to know some of the other queens I'll be working with this year during our training week in Orlando."

"What has been the most fun so far this year?"

"I really have enjoyed the supermarkets. It's a great way to get to talk with people and tell them how versatile the watermelon is. Not many people know what all this fruit can do. I get to share that. It really has me excited about the national supermarket road trip to different Fresh grocery stores our organization has planned later this summer."

"Tell us more about it, please."

"Each queen will visit thirty stores in ten days. Check out our website to see which locations each queen will be at." I turn to look at the camera. "America, I hope to see you there."

"Fun," Stormy says. "What else did you learn during your training in Orlando?"

"I was lucky enough to work with Chef Michael. He taught us all how to carve a watermelon. Later in the segment, I'll be doing that for you."

"Is it difficult to carve a watermelon?"

"No more difficult than a pumpkin. You'll see just how easy it is in a moment. It's all about the tools you use."

Stormy turns and looks at the camera.

"Up next, Grace is going to put some of those carving skills to good use. We'll be back after this commercial break."

The cameramen start moving the cameras to the table area. Stormy ushers me along with her.

"Grace, you're a natural."

"Thanks." I shrug my shoulders a little awkwardly, not knowing what else to say to the compliment.

"So, what are you going to be carving?" Stormy asks, while putting a white apron on.

"A Panda bear face. It's one of the easier designs that can be done in the time we have."

Mrs. Baron brings over my watermelon apron with the Midwest Watermelon Association logo on it. I tie it on quickly because the cameraman is counting down again. Without skipping a beat, Stormy starts the segment.

"For those of you just tuning in, we're here with Grace Summer, the Midwest Watermelon Queen. She's going to show us how to turn this watermelon into a panda bear."

"I am, and the first thing you folks at home want to remember is to find a side of the melon that is the flattest. You need a good, solid base, like the one I have here."

I position the melon in front of the camera and show them the base. I go through the motions of what to do and answer Stormy's questions as she directs them to me. I finish the last step and present my panda bear to the camera. The camera zooms in on my finished product, while Stormy thanks me for being on the show. Then, she signs off with her audience, and the cameras go dark. I shake her hand and the production chief's hand, too, thanking them for the opportunity. Mrs. Baron joins the group, and she and Stormy talk about what the next segment should be about.

We head straight to the car to make it to our next stop, which is for taping some radio commercials for our local watermelon salsa challenge that's coming at the end of the month. Those are easy peasy. The marketing board writes them up, and I just have to say them into the radio's microphone, and I'm done. We swing through a drive-thru and pick up fried chicken and the works for lunch.

Warren texts me on the ride back home.

I saw you on TV today. You did great.

Thanks. Doing anything fun tonight? I text back.

Talking to my girl. Are you back to the office yet?

That stops me a little bit. Warren is great, and I'm really starting to like him, but I don't know what to do with this long-distance thing. I leave the "my girl" part alone and answer his question instead.

Almost. Why?

You'll see.

I don't have long to wait. Mrs. Baron turns the corner, and I see him there, waiting, leaning against the truck.

"It's Warren!" I'm excited to see him, and now his texts make sense.

"I wondered if he might be here. John and Mr. Hartley had a meeting planned for today. They're working on some national convention details."

The car is still rolling to a stop when I fly out the door and throw my arms around Warren. Then I panic. We've never really talked about what this is. What we are. What if he didn't want me to hug him? I tense for a moment, until I calm down enough to feel Warren hugging me back.

"That was a nice greeting."

"It was, wasn't it? Maybe I should have made you work harder."

"In that case, I brought you something."

"You did?"

He pulls out a small box.

"Open it," he tells me.

"Pearl earrings! They're beautiful. Thanks, Warren."

"You're welcome. Here, let me take your bag, so you can put them on."

I hand him my stuff and quickly put the earrings in.

"Are you here for long?"

"No, just today. We have to fly out later tonight."

Mrs. Baron invites the Hartley men for lunch. Mr. Baron and Mr. Hartley talk mostly about the national convention. Mrs. Baron flutters around the table, refilling drinks and making sure everyone's plate stays loaded. Beau and I are still in a standoff. Neither one of us is willing to be the first to bend, so Beau sulks at the table, only opening his mouth to eat his food.

"So, Warren, what have you been up to?" Bennett asks.

"Not much—just working on the farm. Dad has me traveling a lot. It's easier for him to stay home and manage the business, while I do the traveling. And you, Bennett?"

"I've been working on some dirt samples when I get a chance. With Dad's leg, we've been a little shorthanded around here."

"Poor Mr. Baron. He's in the office, and I'm in the packing shed," I add to the conversation.

"They have you working, huh?" Warren asks.

"I like it. It's like old times."

"Yeah, when she would play terrible music and make our eardrums bleed," Bennett says.

"Whatever. I saw you dancing to it."

Bennett and Warren laugh, and we all quickly clear the table.

"Grace, you've worked hard this morning. I think you and Warren should go do something," says Mrs. Baron. She winks at me. That's all the encouragement I need.

I look up at Warren. "Want to get some mint chocolate chip?"

"Ice cream is a weakness of mine. I'm in."

I grab my keys and head to the old farm truck. We drive to our local ice cream parlor. We get our double scoops. I buy. I don't want to be one of those girls who just lets a boy pay on principle. I mean, Warren just bought me pearl earrings; the least I can do is buy the guy some ice cream.

We walk down Main Street and by the old movie theater. They've converted it into a church now, so the kiosk advertises Sunday service times instead of movie shows.

"Interesting. I wouldn't have thought to use it for that."

"Yeah, it's been a lot of things. I think they're just using it until their building is finished."

"That makes sense."

Warren stops in front of the Red Skelton Museum sign, advertising one of Red Skelton's old films. "Come on. Let's go in."

He takes my hand and pays for our tickets. The seats are old-timey, and the room smells a little musty, but the show's funny. I snuggle down next to Warren, enjoying just being near him. Before I'm ready, the show is over, and it's time to head back. The ride back to the farm goes too fast, even though I take every country road I can think of.

"I had fun today," I say.

"Me, too. Remind me to surprise you more often."

"Gladly," I answer, pulling into the office driveway.

Mr. Hartley and Mr. Baron are on the front door step. Mrs. Baron must be at the packing shed, or she would have forced Mr. Baron to be sitting. He wobbles a little on his crutches when he tries to shake Mr. Hartley's hand.

Warren brushes a strand of hair off my face and says, "I'll see you at MAP, Grace. I know you'll be busy, but I'd like to take you on a real date."

"I'd like that, too." I can't stop the smile that spreads across my face.

"Great! I'll text you later. I have to go, or we'll miss our plane."

He pats my knee and jogs to the rental car. I lean back in the seat. As Gramps would say, today was a day for the books. My appearances were successful; Warren surprised me with a visit and gave me earrings; and he asked me on a real date.

Chapter 10

"YOU'LL BE GONE FOR TWO months!"

I can't stop myself from shouting. Gramps and I are walking to the cemetery to put flowers on the headstones. When I was little, I used to think of it as a sea of gray stone. It seemed like it went on forever. We've come here a lot over the years. It used to be just to visit Grandma, but now there are three more stones besides hers.

"Grace, I need to go. The pastor who was going to go just got really sick. He won't be strong enough for the trip. Besides, your busy season will be starting with the Midwest Watermelon Association."

We sit on a bench under the oak tree. Usually, we tell stories we remember about Grandma, Mom, Dad, and Luke. Not today, though. I'm too busy coming to terms with Gramps going halfway around the world.

"They need me."

"So do I." I can't keep the frustration out of my voice.

"I know you think I'm abandoning you, but I think it will be good for you. In some ways, I think I'm holding you back." He lets out a sigh.

"It's what I'm called to do," he gently reminds me.

Gramps is right. It *is* his calling to help other people. I'm being selfish, but two months without him is a long time. I remind myself that I'll be really busy. Besides, he's a pastor. I can't stand in his way.

"Gramps, you have to go. I know that. I just . . . well, I don't want to go back to that dark place." My throat feels like it's closing in a little bit, but I keep talking. "You know I've been getting better. I really, really don't want to backslide, Gramps."

"I understand that. You won't. Mrs. Baron will take good care of you. Besides, I'll be just a phone call away."

"We can thank Mrs. Baron for that," I smirk, feeling a little bit better.

"Ha, she will keep me updated if you don't."

Leaving for MAP, the largest produce advertising convention of the year, is more difficult than normal. I said goodbye to Gramps this morning, knowing he'll be gone on his mission trip when I get back. And now, because the boys out-muscled me, I'm the smooshed middle of a Bennett and Beau sandwich. Mr. and Mrs. Baron are somewhere else on the plane, or the boys never would have gotten away with it.

"Are you really that upset about the middle seat?" Bennett asks.

He shoves his black carry-on bag beside mine in the overhead compartment.

"No, just thinking about Gramps being gone for two months," I grumble, unable to keep a soft sob from coming out at the end.

Bennett takes his seat and clinks the metal pieces of the seatbelt, tightly fastening them together.

"Don't worry. We'll take care of you," Bennett says.

"Oh, like you did today when you did *not* give me the aisle seat?"

The flight attendant walks by, checking our seatbelts and closing the overhead compartments.

"Come on, Grace, my legs are double the length of yours," Bennett says.

Beau grumbles something under his breath, so I glare at him. Still not feeling any better, I stick my tongue out at him, too. It didn't work. I'm still angry, so I decide I do have something to say to him after all.

"Really, after barely saying two words to each other for nearly two weeks, the first thing you can come up with is grumbling under your breath. Very mature, Beau."

"Yes, you, too. Sticking your tongue out at me—very mature."

The fasten seat belt sign comes on, cutting off any more of our conversation, so I just roll my eyes at him instead. He makes me so mad. I just want to shake him.

Within five minutes we are rocketing towards the sky, Bennett reading a book about soil conservation and Beau shuffling through his phone. I try to ignore him as best as I can, seeing how both boys seem to let their legs creep into my space. Flying doesn't really bother me; but I can't sleep on planes, so I grab my fashion magazine, trying to zone out. There's a really interesting article about mixing colors and patterns I've been saving for the plane ride.

Thirty minutes into the flight, I'm stuck. Bennett's head has landed on my shoulder again. I gently push him back into his seat. On the other side of me, Beau leans his arm and head on my armrest. I can't even turn the pages of my magazine. I remind myself that each one of these trips puts money in my bank account for college, so I suck it up and only imagine throat punching them, instead of actually doing it. Landing in New Orleans and getting in our hotel room can't come quickly enough.

The ride in the stainless-steel elevator from our twelfth-floor rooms is done in silence, except for the elevator music floating through the air. While Mr. Baron's mood has gotten drastically better now that he can hobble around, he's still not a hundred percent, and the walk from the suite to the elevator doors reminded him of that. Mrs. Baron adjusts my crown and sash one more time, and Mr. Baron shifts his weight, leaning on his cane, clearly annoyed to be using it.

The elevator doors open to the convention center. The entire complex is about two football fields wide. Vendors line up in booths, showing the latest technologies for farmers, producers, and brokers. Anyone who is involved with produce is here. For the next three days, they will be on display for everyone to see. It's one of the largest events our organization participates in. The marketing board gets a booth, but, then, all of the individual organizations have them, too. This year, the Midwest Watermelon Association has decided to show different types of recipes that involve grilled watermelon.

Mr. Baron and the boys head to the marketing board's booth, while Mrs. Baron and I follow the vendor map to find ours. The set-up crew did a great job. There's green AstroTurf down, and we have several board members grilling watermelon on the spot. Large banners hang on each side of our display with the words "Midwest

Watermelon Association" in bright red. Tables are set up with red and white checkered tablecloths. Mrs. Baron's special watermelon salsa gets dolloped on top, so I can hand it out to the people milling around the convention center. The main goal for today is to let people see how versatile the fruit really is. I've been smiling and talking to people with Mrs. Baron all morning when Warren stops by. I can't stop my eyes from lighting up, giving away just how happy I am to see him.

"Hi, you."

"I'm glad I found you." He holds up the convention center map. "This place is crazy crowded."

"I know. I've been handing out watermelon samples all morning, and it doesn't look to be slowing down."

"Have you eaten yet?" he asks.

"No."

"There is a food court—if you'd like to go, and it's okay with Mrs. Baron."

"Sure, go ahead. We'll hold down the fort," she says.

"Thanks. We'll bring you something back," I promise.

Warren looks good, as always, in his dark denim jeans and light red, button-down shirt, with his sleeves rolled up to the elbow. The left chest has "Hartley Farms" embroidered on it. People stare as we walk by. I'm sure we make a striking picture—Warren looking like he walked out of a Hollister ad and me with my crown and sash.

We walk by the Northwest Watermelon Association booth. V gives me a thumb's up when she sees us. She's handing out pamphlets by a video screen that's showing the planting process of the seedlings.

"So, I missed you," he remarks casually.

Warmth spreads through my chest. "Me, too. I really like spending time with you."

"I was hoping to ask you to go on a real date."

"You were?"

"So, is that a yes?"

"Technically, you haven't asked me yet."

He gives me a sideways grin.

"Grace Summer, will you go on a date with me?"

"Yes."

"Okay. I'll pick you up tonight. Eight work?"

"Sounds like it will."

We make it to the food court and settle on cheeseburgers and fries. I take a bite, ready for some greasy comfort food.

"So, what do you want to do tonight?" he asks.

"Let's go to Frenchmen Street," I suggest.

"Sounds good."

We make our way back to my booth—neither one of us in a hurry to get there. It's like we've had only these brief snapshots of time together, and neither one of us wants this one to end.

All too quickly, we make it back. Mrs. Baron is in full-swing, handing out watermelon. I take over for her, and Warren hands her the cheeseburger.

"Thanks." She takes the offered food and grabs a seat.

"Mrs. Baron, I would like to take Grace out tonight if that would be okay with you."

She eyeballs him for a bit before saying, "You two may go, but not alone. You both know the rules for the watermelon queens."

She looks directly at me when she speaks, making me feel guilty.

"I'll see if some of the other girls want to go," I offer.

"John and Bennett are headed back tomorrow, so Beau and Bennett can go with you guys tonight," Mrs. Baron says.

I stifle a groan. Beau and I still aren't really talking to one another, and the thought of having them both tag along to watch my every move stinks, but I give the expected "yes, ma'am," response.

Warren and I continue to work the front part of the booth, handing out grilled watermelon samples to the passersby.

"I'll try to round up some of the girls to go with us tonight. That will be better than just having the boys with us."

"Good call. Want to meet in the hotel lobby at eight?" Warren asks.

"That will be best."

"I'll see you then," he says before heading back into the crowd.

"Warren?"

"Yes?"

"I'm sorry about tonight."

"Me too, pretty girl. I'll see you tonight."

I watch him walk away and start formulating my plan for tonight.

I text V.

Want to go out tonight?

Sure.

I need a favor.

Spill it, girl. What do you need?

A diversion. Get all the queens together.

If this works, Bennett and Beau won't know what hit them.

Warren is waiting with the rest of the queens as the boys and I head toward the lobby. He's in the middle of the group, telling some sort of joke that has everyone laughing. Obviously, he's very comfortable being the center of attention.

Bennett falters a little when he sees Noelle.

"You didn't tell me she'd be here."

"You didn't ask." Bennett sees the gleam in my eyes, which pretty much lets him know I had it planned the whole time.

Noelle looks amazing in her gray skinny jeans, white shirt, and light pink leather jacket, but Bennett's biggest issue is that she can't stand him. I'd say the feeling is mutual for Bennett.

"Suck it up, Bennett," Beau says, giving Bennett a punch in the arm.

Bennett punches back.

"You two, stop." I wedge myself in between them, so they'll quit. "Having you two here was your mom's idea. Not mine."

"Let's just get it over with," Beau says.

I stop and turn to face them.

"If you two embarrass me tonight, I'll punch you both myself. Got it?"

I turn and walk toward the group, not bothering to look back. They'll follow. They've both already made it clear they plan to ruin my night. Stupid boys.

Warren meets me and gives me a hug and then keeps his arm slung around my shoulders.

"Grace, you look amazing," V says.

"You, too, girl. I have to borrow that sometime."

"You girls look great, too." I motion to Audrey, Rosanne, and Becca.

I stop when my eyes land on Noelle. Noelle and Bennett are squared off, their body language screaming displeasure.

"Bennett," Noelle says.

"They didn't tell me you were going to be here." He breaks the silence and manages to insult her at the same time.

"Let's just try to avoid one another the best we can."

"Agreed," Bennett says.

"Wow, the first thing you two have agreed on. Tonight could be magical." I try to cut the tension by being funny. Unfortunately, neither one of them are feeling it.

"The limo's here," Warren says, completely ignoring my attempt at humor.

We all hop in and roll the windows down to take in the night air. The driver drops us off on Frenchmen Street and heads off to find a place to park. He gives Warren his phone number before he leaves, though.

"This is awesome," Audrey says.

Dance music pulsates through the air.

"Come on, boys, we want to dance," V says.

We make it to the dance floor of the under-twenty-one club and start dancing. Beau and Bennett stand on either side of Warren.

"Those boys drive me nuts," I grumble. "V, we have to do something."

"I got you, girl." Then she looks at Noelle. "Which Baron boy do you want?"

"I'm not taking either one of them," she pronounces.

"Please, you have to help me. They are guarding me like watchdogs."

"Fine. I'll take Bennett, but you owe me."

"You're the best." I throw my arms around her in a quick hug.

"So, what's the plan?" Noelle asks, looking at V.

"Just keep the boys busy," V tells her; then she looks at me.

"Meet me in the bathroom, Grace. There's another way out the back. I'll tell Warren where to meet you," V says.

Noelle heads to Bennett to keep up her end of the plan. I head to the bathroom, so V can pull Warren onto the dance floor to tell him our plan. Out of sight, I head down the club's kitchen hallway. Warren catches up with me before I'm out the back door.

"I'm impressed, Grace," he says in a hushed tone.

"Did we lose them?" I look back over my shoulder to make sure no one is following us.

"I'd say we're safe."

We head down the street. Different vendors show us their wares, and music from the different clubs blares out to the street.

"It's dirtier than I thought it would be." I look around the street, surprised to see so much grime covering everything.

"Yes, I should have taken you to the nicer part of the French quarter. The buildings are beautiful there," he claims, tapping my nose with his finger.

"It's okay. I wanted to see what all the fuss was about down here, anyway."

We walk hand-in-hand, not really caring where we go. I stop and buy some strings of beads and a few postcards to show Gramps when he gets back.

"When do you fly out tomorrow?" I ask, as we head toward the club we snuck away from. Noelle is going to kill me already for being gone this long.

"Early morning. Grace, before we go back, there was something I was hoping to do."

"What's that?" I turn my face up to his expectantly.

He turns to face me and takes my other hand. In that second, I realize he's going to kiss me. My stomach and chest tighten in anticipation. With the accident and then trying to screw my head back on straight, I never got around to kissing a boy. Warren's head moves closer, so I close my eyes, lifting my face to meet his.

"Grace, what are you doing?"

Bennett's voice shatters the moment, and with it any hope of getting my first kiss tonight. I turn to find the entire group staring at me in various degrees of interest.

"Sorry. I tried to keep them busy, but Noelle wasn't helping very much with Bennett," V says.

Bennett looks at Noelle accusingly.

"I wondered what your angle was."

"And I thought my acting was so convincing." Sarcasm drips from her voice.

Unwilling to let her one up him, Bennett shoots back, "Not by a long shot, sweetheart."

"I'm not your sweetheart," she snaps back, loathing written all over her face.

"While this is all very entertaining," Beau interrupts, "let's get back to why we're all out here in the first place."

Bennett turns to look at me. "Mom would kill us," he points between himself and Beau, "if she knew we let you out of our sight on Frenchmen Street. Grace, what were you thinking?"

"Nothing. You two are driving me crazy. Besides, I wasn't alone."

I raise my hand, intertwined with Warren's, for emphasis.

"Warren was a perfect gentleman."

Beau snorts, while Bennett just stands there with his hands in his pockets and says, "I'm happy to hear that he was, but this is mostly about the contract you signed. If you like Warren—"

"I've heard enough. We're leaving," Beau says. "I'll get us a cab."

"I'd say the decision is Grace's," Warren says.

I give Warren's hand a squeeze. "That's okay. I'll go with them."

He looks down at me, so I smile at him.

"It's getting late, anyway. I should go. As much as I liked spending time with you tonight, we shouldn't have snuck away."

"As long as that's what you want," he replies.

"It is. Thanks for the walk." I give him a quick hug.

"Anytime," he says.

I walk to the cab silently, preparing for battle. The boys are going to get an earful when we get in. Bennett slides in first. I follow, and Beau slides in last and closes the door.

"The Plaza, please," Bennett says.

"You guys are smothering me," I shout.

They each move a little closer to their side of the cab.

"That's not what I meant. You guys have to ease up. If your mom knew—"

"If she *knew* you were out there alone, Mom would kill us. And then you," Bennett counters, raising his voice as he goes.

"I. Was. Not. Alone."

"Close enough," Beau grumbles, anger clearly written across his face.

"If you two weren't so annoying and judgmental, maybe I wouldn't have had to give you the slip. Besides, do you have any proof that Warren's a bad guy?"

They both sit there, looking down at the floor.

"I thought not. So, you two will just shut it and leave me and Warren alone. Until you have any real proof, I don't want to hear it. Got it?" I demand.

They say nothing, and neither do I for the rest of the ride to the hotel. Bennett pays the driver, and I head up to my room and start packing for the early plane ride home tomorrow.

Chapter 11

MORNING IN THE FIELDS IS my favorite time of the day. The sun is just about to rise, and all of the workers are fanning out to the rows of watermelons. I turn the key and hear the chug of the tractor as it comes to life. Then, I shift it into gear. The wheels roll forward as I settle onto the old, yellow seat. There are places where the fabric is missing and, in some places, duct-taped.

It's too early to start the music just yet; but my coffee warms my insides, and I begin the slow drive down the row, careful not to crush the vines with the tractor wheels. The watermelons are coming off the vines like crazy, which is good because tomorrow is Mrs. Baron's watermelon salsa-making day for the farmer's market. My two wagons are full after the end of only one row. I unhitch the wagons and call for a few of the crew members to help me put two more wagons on the back of the tractor. The workers fan out and begin the process again. Beau and his crew are working in the field next to mine. Eventually, Bennett pulls up with empty wagons, hooks up Beau's full wagons and the ones my crew filled to his tractor, and heads back to the packing shed.

We are in full production mode, so we stagger lunch breaks. Beau and I keep going, eating our sandwiches on the tractor, while the crews switch out. Raul brings the converted school bus, which is basically an old school bus with the sides cut out and the bench seats removed. The new crew unloads from the bus, spilling out and taking over the rows from the crew in the field, so they can climb in and head back for their lunch break.

Driving the tractor today leaves me time to think about Warren and our trip to New Orleans. I so wanted that kiss with Warren. When we got home from the promotion, there were roses waiting for me. The boys didn't say anything, but then again, they've pretty much stayed away from me after the yelling tornado I was in the cab. Any way I look at it, I was justified, though. I stop the tractor, while waiting for the crew to load the melons on the wagon, and I snap a picture of me driving the tractor for Warren and send it with a text message.

Hi.

He texts back right away.

Wow! Great pic. Makes me miss you more.

His words make me go all warm and gooey inside.

Miss you, too. Sorry gotta go. In the fields now.

Warren doesn't text back. He's worked enough to know that when in the fields, everything else takes second place.

The sun is just starting to drop on the horizon when we finish the field and use the CB to call the packing shed for pick up. Several of the crew members take off toward the pond for a quick splash before they head home for the night. Beau is already at the edge of the pond when I walk up. He's facing the water, talking to a few of the younger workers. He doesn't see me, so I sneak behind him and shove him in the water. He comes up sputtering.

"I told you I'd get even for your little trick in New Orleans," I call triumphantly, with my hands on my hips, which makes everyone laugh even harder.

"I guess we're even now," he says, slowly wading toward the bank.

I stand there, arms crossed and gloating as he sloshes out of the water. I step to the side, realizing too late I should have never let him get this close after what I just did. He scoops me up and carries me over his shoulder into the water. Everyone whoops and hollers when I come up for air.

"Oh, it's on now," I sputter, dunking him under one more time and then swimming away. I splash some of the workers who were egging him on, and before long, everyone's joining in the fun.

We all climb out when the old, red school bus pulls up. The seats have been removed, and the sides have been cut out to accommodate putting watermelons into it. At the end of the day, it doubles as transportation to take the crews back to the packing shed. Bennett takes one look at Beau and me and says, "You two dry off first before you get in the new truck."

Beau gives a fake salute to Bennett's back.

"Yes, sir," he retorts, obviously annoyed.

"Doing okay?" I goad him a little.

"Typical Bennett, thinking people can't think for themselves," he says, breaking open a watermelon for us to share.

I take a big hunk out of the heart of the melon. The juice slides down my arm, but I don't care. It's part of the fun of eating one directly from the fields. Seriously, we should just sell the juice. It's so good.

"I know what you mean. It must be a Baron-genetics thing." I look over at him to see if he caught my dig.

Beau sighs.

"You are such a pain in my side sometimes, Grace."

He sounds angry, like it's my fault.

"What did I ever do to you?"

"Look, can we not talk about it right now?"

"No. I *want* answers," I demand.

He looks out across the pond, saying nothing. Closing me out.

"Fine, I'll go first." I lean forward, angry at him for being so stubborn. "Most of the time, you act like you can't stand me or that I'm a pain, but then you won't let Warren get close to me either. Which is it, Beau?"

I'm getting angrier with each word that comes out of my mouth. He stands up, with his hands on his hips.

"Why do you push me so hard?" I ground out, while shooting straight up.

"You want to know why?" he replies.

"Yes!" I yell back.

Beau steps forward and throws his arms out to his sides.

"Warren's no good for you. You deserve better; and when I see you with him, I know Luke would hate it."

"It's always about Luke with you." I can't help it. I yell, frustration bouncing around inside of me. "I'm tired of this being about Luke!"

"Well, sorry, but it is. Looking at you reminds me of Luke. I see him in you all of the time. He was my best friend, you know."

"Your best friend? Well, he was *my brother*!" I shout, tears sliding down my face. "So, if you could just tell me what this is really about, I'd appreciate it."

"Okay, fine . . . I hate it! Is that what you wanted to hear?" He all but yells.

"You hate it?" I'm totally confused. "What is that supposed to mean?" I don't even know what to do with that information. Beau looks deflated.

He stands there for a few minutes before he whispers, "I was the first one at the accident. I'm the one who pulled you two out and did the chest compressions to save you. Luke was alive when I pulled him out but barely hanging on. He kept asking for you. I went back to the car and got you out. You weren't breathing."

Beau pauses for a moment, swallowing hard, and looks out over the pond.

"Luke grabbed my arm and begged me to take care of you first. I left his side to do compressions. Once your heart was beating again, I went back to him, but he was dead, and no matter what I did, my best friend wasn't coming back."

He hangs his head but not before I can see the tortured look in his eyes.

Suddenly, the truth hits me, and I can't breathe. The pain is deafening. I crumple to the ground in a heap. Everything I remember from that night crashes down on my chest.

"No one told me it was you," I whisper.

"It doesn't matter." He looks like a wounded animal, and I have no idea what to do to make it any better. There's just too much new information floating around in my head. "There's more to the story, but we're dry now, and it's getting late. Let's get you home."

I don't argue. He looks wrung out, and, honestly, so am I. I don't know that I could handle more right now, anyway. I walk to the truck, weighed down with memories and the new information swimming around inside my head. Beau shuts my door as I lean back in the truck seat.

We ride in silence for a while before the fact that I might not be here if it wasn't for Beau comes crashing back to the front of my mind.

"Beau?"

"Yeah?"

"Thanks for saving my life." It feels inadequate, like I should do some grand gesture. My mind comes up blank.

Instead, I try to get him to do some of the talking. "You said there was more."

Beau glances over at me, then pulls the truck onto the gravel road. The gravel makes a crunching sound as the wheels continue to move toward the farm house.

"I want to try to explain why I act the way I do with you."

"I would like that." My insides churn, and I feel a little guarded. What if he tells me something that I can't handle right now?

"Okay, just hear me out," he takes a deep breath. "In eighth grade, I noticed you. And by noticed, I mean, I felt something for you. I told Luke, but he told me to stay away from you–which I did. But the feelings have never really gone away. Now, when I look at you, I see Luke and hate myself because he's not here. How could I be into the one girl who kind of took him away from me? But I can't stand by and let you be with a guy who doesn't deserve you. Grace, what I'm trying to say, is that I'm the way I am with you because I'm angry with myself for being into you."

I don't know what to say. What does that even mean? Thankfully, we have just pulled up to the office. I jump out of the truck and head for my car. Beau follows after me.

"Grace, wait!"

I turn to face him.

"What are you thinking?" he asks.

"I don't know," I answer, looking anywhere but at him. Instead, I run to the safety of my car.

Confusion swirls around in my head. In one sentence, he confesses he's into me, but hates himself for it. He blames me for Luke's death. Well, he should stay on board that train because I do, too. But why is he bringing all of this up now when I'm finally starting to climb out of that hole of depression? All of a sudden, I'm furious at him for doing this to me.

I stop my retreat. Turning to face him, it's all I can do not to yell at this point. "You know what, Beau? I *do* know what I'm thinking, and it's that you're a jerk for trying to get in my head this way."

"I'm not trying to get in your head."

"It just seems like you are. Why would you tell me all of that about the accident now? Was it to make me feel vulnerable? Or that I owe you something?" I am so angry and confused, I'm shaking.

Beau just stands there, anger flashing in his eyes.

"Just leave me alone." I stomp my foot to relieve some of the crazy emotions rolling around inside.

"In case you missed it, I was just trying to explain my feelings to you," he bursts out.

I brush past him and grab the car door handle and open it. "Oh, I didn't miss what you were *trying* to do," I ground out.

"I'm not going to stand by and let you get hurt." He takes a step toward me, but I hold my ground.

"Too late. You already did. It's not Warren you should be worried about, but *you*!" I shout.

His eyes register hurt or anger. I can't tell which.

"I'm not trying to hurt you. I'm trying to protect you, but you're so stubborn that—"

"You make me so mad," I cut him off.

Beau puts his hand on my open door. "The feeling's mutual. But, I will make sure Warren doesn't hurt you. I owe that much to Luke."

I stomp my foot on the ground, trying to release more anger. "No!"

"What do you mean no?" he asks, arms folded over his chest.

"Seriously, Beau, God gave you too much in the looks department and not enough in the brains department," I all but shout.

I realize what I just said as soon as the look on Beau's face changes to surprise.

Embarrassment heats up my cheeks.

He takes another step toward me.

I put my hand up to stop him.

"Don't read into it. I also think dogs are cute, so don't get too excited."

Beau grins his sideways grin, making me blush brighter.

"Just butt out of my relationship with Warren."

I sit in my driver's seat and try to close the door. Beau has his hand still on it, so the only reason I am able to close it is because he basically shuts it for me.

I really need to talk with Gramps, but he's half a world away. I could call, but I'd get voicemail, so I don't bother.

Instead, I take the long way home, trying to figure this all out. Why didn't anyone tell me about Beau saving my life? And do I believe him that he's had a thing for me since eighth grade? All I know is that it seems pretty remarkable that he's telling me all this now. It's almost like he's trying to mess with my head and talk me out of dating Warren by making it seem like he's interested. He's had four years to say something. Why now? It doesn't make sense.

On the other hand, how do I feel about Beau? Do I want him to like me? That's the million-dollar question. Then it hits me; Beau is getting exactly what he wanted, making me think about someone else and second-guessing my feelings for Warren.

Chapter 12

I'VE BEEN CHOPPING CILANTRO FOR the better part of fifteen minutes when the boys start bringing in the watermelons for the salsa.

"Where you want these, Mom?" Bennett asks.

"By the counter," Mrs. Baron says.

Bennett and Beau start stacking them, while she watches to make sure they're stacked in rows of four. Seeing Beau reminds me of last night's fight. He's been giving me a wide berth all morning. Honestly, I'm glad. I'm not really ready to call a truce, but having to work together today stinks.

When the melons are all in, she puts all three of us to work chopping the melons into small, square pieces. I take out my frustration with Beau on the watermelon, quickly slicing and chopping the meat of the fruit.

"Whoa, Grace. Doing okay?" Bennett asks.

"Yup." I continue to chop away.

"Well, then, stop chopping so hard, dear. You'll smash the melon, instead of making nice, diced pieces," Mrs. Baron says.

I force myself to slow down my chopping and to stop slamming the knife down so hard on the cutting board. Beau wisely keeps his mouth closed and his eyes on his own board.

"I'd say something's wrong," Bennett says, pulling on the red bandana tied around my head.

Mrs. Baron tsks but doesn't say anything else. She heads to the screened-in porch to fill her first set of jars for the farmer's market today.

"Did you have a fight with Warren?" he asks.

I don't say anything, hoping he'll just let it drop. No such luck.

"It is Warren."

I say nothing.

"I'm right."

I still ignore him and keep working on the watermelon.

"You finally realized what a loser he is. Huh? 'Bout time. Yes!" Bennett says, punching his arm and knife straight up in the air.

"Cool it with the knife, will you?"

Bennett puts the knife down but keeps punching his fists in the air like he's won first prize at the fair.

"You know, for a college boy, you're not very mature," I point out.

"I can live with that."

He does his signature eyebrow wiggle and then leans down, still acting like an idiot. "So, tell me all about it, girlfriend," he uses a high-pitched, girly voice.

"You're not my girlfriend. It's *not* happening."

"I can keep a secret," he whispers loudly.

"She said no. Bennett, shut up," Beau says.

"When do you take Grace's side? Now I have to know."

"NO!" Beau and I shout at the same time.

Bennett looks between us.

"Oh, this just got a whole lot more interesting." Bennett makes another annoying face, while tapping his fingers together in excitement.

Beau and I go back to chopping, while Bennett continues to try to get us to spill it. Finally, Mrs. Baron comes back in the room, which puts an end to Bennett's digging for details.

"Mrs. Baron, there's a lot of juice left in the bottom of our bowls. Would you mind if we saved it, so I can drink it later?"

"Sure, Grace," she agrees.

"That's actually a really good idea," Bennett says, giving me a high-five.

"I think it would sell at the market, too," I add.

"Let's do some test batches and see what people say," Bennett suggests.

We gather the remaining jars and fill them with the juice. Mrs. Baron adds a little red and white checkered cloth over the lids for decoration, and we add them to the truck.

The farmer's market is already busy when we get there. Vendors are setting up their produce and baked goods. Mr. Kelly has his chicken eggs out and a few baby chicks for sale. I've wanted chickens for as long as I can remember. I wave at Mr. Kelly and extract a promise from him not to sell all the baby chicks until I at least get to hold one. Mrs. Baron puts her dark green tablecloth down and starts unloading her first batch of watermelon salsa. Mrs. Baron and I stay to work the market, while the boys head back to the farm to work with Mr. Baron.

It doesn't take long before she has to send me to the refrigerated truck to get another batch. When I get back, the juice we made is almost gone.

"People love the juice, Grace. This could be a great side business for the farm," Mrs. Baron says.

"Really?"

"Yes, we'll talk to John about it when we get home."

"Okay." A million ideas start running through my head. The watermelon organization is always looking for new ways to market the watermelon. This could totally be one.

Customers steadily stream to Mrs. Baron's table, but we're not so busy that we can't talk.

"You know, Grace, I don't really like to meddle, but I have heard some things about Warren that make me wonder."

"Did Bennett and Beau tell you these things?" I ask, trying to keep the frustration out of my voice. What is it with these people? I finally find a boy I like, and all they can say is how terrible he is. It's getting old. Fast.

"And other people," Mrs. Baron says, sounding guilty.

"Uh-huh." That's all I'm going to give her on that one.

"Well, sweetie, we all care about you and just don't want to see you get hurt is all."

"I know you do." I put more jars of salsa on the table. "It's just that I like Warren, and he seems to like me. Beau is driving me crazy about it."

"Is he now? Hmmm, I wondered when he would realize he likes—"

"No, ma'am. It's not like that. He's appointed himself my guardian in Luke's place, says he owes Luke that much. Besides, Bennett is doing the same thing."

"I won't say any more about it," she promises. "But what boy would go to that much trouble if he didn't care for the girl? I'll leave you to think on it while I go get another batch of salsa."

Think on it? No, not going to. Warren is a good guy. I like Warren. Why is it so hard for people to figure that out? Beau is a jerk. He does annoying things and keeps getting in the way with Warren. Does he have ulterior motives? The only thing I've figured out when Mrs. Baron gets back to the booth is that the Baron boys are a pain.

The farmer's market slows down as it becomes evening, so we call it a night. Packing up the truck is done pretty easily, since all of the salsa was sold. My overalls pocket is full of twenty percent of the profit. Mrs. Baron wouldn't take no for an answer. On the drive back, she invites me to stay for supper, so we can talk to Mr. Baron about my juice idea. I agree. The alternative is a turkey sandwich and a movie by myself, anyway.

Mrs. Baron parks the truck, and we head into the kitchen through the back door. She begins pulling things out of the freezer.

"What can I help with?"

"The biscuits, for now. Then, maybe we can throw together a pie."

She hands me the roll of biscuits. I place them on the pan and put them in to the oven. Mrs. Baron places the recipe for her apple pie in front of me.

"Remember your way around my kitchen?" she asks.

"I got it." I start heading to the pantry for the flour and apples.

Carrying my supplies back, it hits me. I should be doing this with Mom. It's a dull ache of a reminder that I'll never have the chance to listen to her laugh again or throw flour at Luke like when we used to help Mom make supper.

"Grace, dear, are you okay? Your face went white and pensive for a minute."

I turn to look at Mrs. Baron, forcing a smile.

"I'm fine. I was just thinking about my mom."

"I was thinking about her earlier today, too. When you thought of the juice idea. She would have been proud of you, you know."

She starts making the iced tea.

"I can't take the place of your mother, but would you let me help you with that pie?"

"I'd like that." I fight back tears, and we begin slicing the apples together.

"I miss my best friend. I've been selfishly keeping you close to me because you remind me of her."

"I do?"

"You've got the same wavy, blonde hair and big blue eyes, shaped just like your mother's. And you've got her strong will, too."

Mrs. Baron's words dull the ache in my chest.

"Thanks."

"Any time," she says, putting the pie in the oven and taking out the biscuits.

We set the table and pour the tea into glasses before the guys come clomping in the back door.

"It smells good, Mom," Bennett says.

"Do I smell apple pie?" Beau asks.

"Grace made it," Mrs. Baron says before Mr. Baron gives her a quick kiss.

Beau looks at me in surprise.

"I only helped." I put my hands in my back pockets, embarrassed.

"I'm happy you're joining us," Mr. Baron says.

"Dinner will be ready soon. Go get cleaned up, boys. You stink," Mrs. Baron says.

The guys quickly head upstairs to take baths. It's kind of funny to see a grown man and two big boys jump to attention when she gives orders. Obviously, the boys love her, and Mr. Baron adores her. Who couldn't? But it's safe to say Mrs. Baron makes all three of her boys toe the line.

The boys heap their plates full of mashed potatoes, green beans, and chicken. The biscuits and blackberry jelly gets passed around, and then Mr. Baron thanks God for our food and a strong harvest. For a little while, there is only the clinking of silverware and glasses as everyone eats.

Mrs. Baron starts the conversation.

"John, today Grace had this great idea about watermelon juice."

"The juice, huh?" he asks, looking at me.

"So, the watermelon juice is one of my favorite parts. I can straight drink it. It got me thinking. Why not sell it? I mean, there's pineapple juice and orange juice. Why can't there be watermelon juice?"

"That's brilliant," Mr. Baron says.

"We packaged some up for you girls today. How'd it go?" Bennett asks.

"It was gone in the first hour." Happy I had good news to share about the juice, I blurt out the news before Mrs. Baron can say anything.

"John, could this be something Melon Ridge Farms does?" Mrs. Baron asks.

"I think so. Let me call some of my friends, but we could use the extra shed to start the bottling process."

"Should you call the promotions board?" Beau asks.

"Good idea. Bennett will get on the phone with Scott Stone after supper. And I'll make the other phone calls."

Mrs. Baron cuts the pie, while Mr. Baron gives us our assignments.

"It will have to be done with a cold press. Beau, Grace, you two get online and figure out where we can buy one. Look into bottling options, too."

Of course, he'd pair me with Beau. I resolve to just forget about what Bennett teased us about earlier and act like it never happened.

"I'll take care of marketing," Mrs. Baron says.

We finish our pie and all head in separate directions.

"Wow, your dad really seems to think this can work," I say to Beau.

"It's a good idea."

I open my eyes wide as we head into the office. "Did Beau Baron just compliment me without being prompted by his mother?"

He smiles his sideways grin. Then his face softens a little. "Listen, Grace, about the other day—"

"Let's act like it never happened," I cut him off, not wanting to think about it.

"If that's what you want." He looks disappointed.

"It is."

"Okay, but I'm still going to protect you from Warren."

"I don't need protecting. I'm a big girl."

Beau starts to say something, but I cut him off again.

"Let's just agree to disagree. Okay?"

"Fine." He turns to the computer, his movements stiff, and searches *industrial cold press*. A full page of options pop up.

"I'll take notes. You just start clicking on the pages." It's going to be a long night, and I still need to get packed for the flight to Washington, D.C., tomorrow.

Chapter 13

WASHINGTON, D.C., HAS ALWAYS BEEN on the agenda for the watermelon queens. But for the Barons and me, it's now a business trip for our new watermelon juice company, too, which means that Raul has been left in charge of the farm again because everyone came to Washington. Mr. Baron gave us all our jobs to do. For him and Bennett, it will mostly be the business side of it. Mrs. Baron and Beau will work on the marketing and bottling and switch off going to promotions with me.

First stop is the Food and Drug Administration building to have a meeting and photo op with the FDA board. The FDA basically makes all of the rules for the food industry to protect the public's health and wellness.

The national organization purchased red, long-sleeved dresses that flow out to the knee for the queens. They have deep, V-neck backs that have red straps crisscrossing the back. The belt of the dress has been made to look like a watermelon. Each girl's dress has her organization's logo embroidered on the left chest.

Mr. Baron is in this meeting, talking with the FDA commissioner in the corner. Mr. Stone is with them, too. There's a lot of handshaking, and then Mr. Baron finds Mrs. Baron to whisper something in her ear that makes her eyes light up. Hopefully, it has to do with the juice, and I'm just thankful Mr. Baron's the one in charge of the rules and regulations part of bottling the juice.

Noelle is across the room, talking to another committee member. We are all spread around the room. Luckily for me, the person I'm with is talking about her job within the committee, so I can give a noncommittal head shake or "that's interesting" every so often and still seem like I'm paying attention, when I'm really just dying to figure out what Mr. Baron told Mrs. Baron.

Someone comes around and gives everyone in the room a slice of watermelon. Flash bulbs snap like fireworks as the queens take a bite of watermelon, with the board members doing the same thing. It's sure to be a stunning picture and on the cover of *Growing Vines Magazine*.

Mr. Stone gives a quick speech about how thankful we all are to spend this time talking with the FDA commissioner and then lets us know the queens are free to go. We all have meetings with our senators and congressmen shortly and don't want to be late. Mr. Stone, as the marketing board's president, stays behind with Mr. Baron to talk about some of the more pressing issues that face the industry. I force myself to wait until Mrs. Baron and I are alone to ask her what Mr. Baron said.

"Did Mr. Baron say anything to you about the watermelon juice?"

"Only that we are a go. I'm going to call the boys now, so they can get the process started. An email will be coming with the regulations, but we could possibly start production by the end of the month."

She presses the phone to her ear and starts giving orders. I walk along, trying to not jump up and down. There are business men and women walking along the streets, and I already draw attention because of my crown and sash. Jumping up and down like a crazy girl wouldn't help anything.

I decide to take off my crown, but leave the sash, and I force myself to go over the talking points I have to talk about with the senators. Anne, from the marketing board, sent all the queens an email earlier this week, so we would be prepared. One: discuss the global trade policies and issues with supply and demand. Two: discuss regulations from the FDA. Three: thank them for their time.

In her bag, Mrs. Baron has brochures, which also outline my talking points, and gifts, if the senators have kids. She hangs up the phone just as we round the corner to our first appointment for the day. We walk through security and show our credentials in order to get into the building. If the guard working the x-ray machine thinks anything about a girl with a crown in her bag, he doesn't show it, letting me pass on to the next guard, who waves the security wand in front of and behind me before he gives us the all-clear.

The building is all old stone and archways, but it's incredible. Large murals hang on the wall, and a huge American flag descends from the middle of a rotunda. We take the staircase with burgundy carpeting to the second floor, where the elevators are. We hit the button for the fourth floor and wait for the ding of the elevators. To kill time, I count the hours until Warren will be in D.C. His plane lands some time tomorrow evening. We are here for five days, so I should be able to spend some time with him, for sure.

The elevator doors ding, and people crowd in shoulder-to-shoulder for our ride up. When we reach Senator Whichmore's office doorway, my stomach drops a little. I stand in the hall, peeking in. It's a big, open room with gold wallpapered walls with two wooden doors on each side wall, making the space look very symmetrical. There is a mahogany desk, stained very dark, in the middle of the room, where a woman who looks to be in her late-forties sits. Her black hair is pulled back in bun. She wears a black suit and black-rimmed glasses.

"Do I speak first, or will she?" I whisper to Mrs. Baron.

"His secretary will lead us to a room to wait for him," she whispers as we walk toward the desk.

"Okay, so I have a minute to stop feeling nervous?"

"It's okay. I'm a little nervous, too."

It's hard to even imagine Mrs. Baron being nervous. I look at her out of the corner of my eye. She looks like she always does in a red and gray suit with a gray, silk blouse and pumps.

The woman at the desk—his secretary, according to the nameplate on her desk—welcomes us and quickly comes from around her desk.

"Welcome, Grace and Pamela. We're happy you're here. Senator Whichmore is on a phone call, but he'll be with you shortly. If you two will follow me this way."

She directs us to a small conference room.

"Have a seat. Can I get you anything?" she asks.

We both decline. I sit, running through my talking points. Mrs. Baron lets me. She pulls out our pamphlet and sets the kids' gifts to the side of her chair.

We don't wait long before Senator Whichmore comes through the door. Mrs. Baron and I stand up.

"Senator Whichmore, it's nice to meet you." I offer him my hand for a handshake.

"Yes, Grace Summer with the Midwest Watermelon Association, what can I do for you?"

"Our biggest concern has to do with the trade policies and supply and demand issues. There's less farmland now than ever before, and with more mouths to feed worldwide, well, you can see where this becomes an issue. We also need to take into account wages of workers and regulations that we must comply with."

He nods.

"I understand what you're saying, but in some ways, my hands are tied."

I take a breath and pray that he can't see my knees knocking together under the table. This conversation went deep. Fast.

Mrs. Baron goes on to show him the pamphlet.

"We have broken down approximately what our costs are to harvest one field of watermelons per worker, as well as what yield we see from that field. As you can see, due to minimum wage and labor laws, which we agree with and are happy to comply with, it makes it hard to compete."

Senator Whichmore looks impressed with us.

"Ladies, you make a very valid point," he agrees. "I will share your thoughts with my fellow representatives."

We spend more time talking about our FDA visit and then thank him for his time. Mrs. Baron quickly snaps a photo of me and Senator Whichmore for *Growing Vines Magazine,* and we head to our next meeting. The remainder of the day is spent in meetings with our representatives. We have varying degrees of cooperation, but by the time Mrs. Baron and I make it to our hotel room, all I want is a bath and something to eat.

I quickly check my messages. There's one from Gramps, asking about D.C., so I leave him a message with a rundown of my day and quickly send Warren a text, too. Then, I head to my bubble bath because tomorrow is all about sightseeing and Warren.

Mrs. Baron agreed to let me go sightseeing with the queens as long as I took Beau along. Bennett was the obvious first choice, but he has meetings all day with Mr. Baron, Mr. Stone, and Noelle. And because I still have a lot of hours to count down until Warren can be here, I can't be picky. Beau and I meet the rest of the girls in the hotel lobby. Beau wears his normal grumpy expression. I, on the other hand, have on skinny jeans, ballet flats, a black and white striped sweater, and a pleasant look on my face.

Rosanne sees us first.

"Beau, wow, you really clean up nice."

He's got on dark jeans and a chambray button down. His hair, a little longer than normal, curls a little at his neck.

Beau nods. "Thanks, ladies. You all look beautiful this morning."

They all smile brightly up at him, clearly fooled by his charm. Seriously, if they only knew the half of it with him . . . But who am I to judge? At first glance, Beau is hot. Not that I would ever tell him. Besides, it will take only a few minutes in his presence today for the girls to see what a jerk he is.

"Where to first?" he asks, pouring on more charm.

Rosanne grabs his arm, saying, "One of the Smithsonian museums would be fun."

We all start towards the doors of the hotel. We plan to walk today. For the most part, it will be faster and cheaper.

"So, this is good," V says beside me.

"What is?"

"Beau being distracted by Rosanne."

I give the required "Yeah," but am unable to sound excited about it.

She looks at me sideways.

"You should be happy. More Warren time, right?"

"True. I just wonder how long it will take before she's seeing the grumpy, rude Beau."

"Grace, he's only like that with you. How he is with us is totally different."

"What? No he's not." I deny it until V's immovable stare makes me start to think maybe it is just me, which leads me to ask, "Why me?"

"That's something you'll have to figure out. I have a good idea, though."

"Well, what's your idea?"

"Nope, you two will have to work it out."

She walks ahead of me and gets in line to pay for the American History Museum's special Andy Warhol exhibit. The rest of the museum is free, but we decided as a group to check out his artwork.

I pull out my wallet, but before I can get any cash out, the attendant tells me I've already been paid for. I look up to see Beau watching me. Why would Beau do that? Probably so I owe him something. That boy drives me nuts. I drag V with me, so I can catch up with Beau to pay him back for my ticket.

"You didn't have to do that." I hold my hand out with a twenty in it.

"Relax. I used the company credit card."

"Okay. Well, thanks, then." I put the cash back in my pocket.

"No problem." He shrugs his shoulder like it's no big deal.

Rosanne stands by him, ready to pounce. This is the most attention she's gotten from a Baron boy; and while they both drive me crazy, the boys are a hot commodity in the watermelon industry. I see the draw for Bennett. The attraction with Beau, I haven't figured out, unless you're into being irritated on a daily basis.

"So, which way are you two headed?" I ask Rosanne, happy at the possibility of not being babysat all day by Beau.

"I thought we'd start with the first thing on the map and just follow it around," she offers.

"Great idea," V says.

"I think we should all go together," Beau says.

"No, we wouldn't want to mess up your date," V says.

That was brilliant on her part. I have Beau right where I want him now, and the look on his face tells me he knows it. He can't be rude to Rosanne. To Mrs. Baron, being rude is inexcusable. He's stuck—for now, at least.

"Have fun." I press my lips together trying to hide my glee.

V and I head in the opposite direction.

"Too bad Noelle couldn't come with us," V says.

"I think she's going to try to catch up with us later."

The exhibit of the First Ladies' inaugural dresses is amazing. The price of the jewelry is crazy, though. I remember watching the TV while Michelle Obama walked out at the inaugural ball. Her dress was stunning. It's even more stunning in person, and the ring and earrings she wore are more than Gramps makes in an entire year.

"So, any word from Warren yet?" V asks.

"Not yet." I frown a little. There's nothing I can do, but I'm frustrated with the situation.

We make our way to some of the other exhibits and check out the ruby slippers from *The Wizard of Oz*. Then, we head to the food court to get something to eat. It looks like everyone had the same idea because the crew is gathered around the table. Beau must have found a way to disentangle himself from Rosanne. She sits on the farthest chair from his, pouting, which is a bummer because now he'll be my shadow.

On the plus side, Noelle and Bennett have joined us. Noelle sees us coming and waves.

"Hey, guys," she says.

"Hi. Did you just get here?" I question her. It's a little weird to see Bennett and Noelle in the same space and having smiles on their faces that aren't forced.

"No, we've been here for a little while," she answers, looking at Bennett.

"Yeah, the meeting finished up early, and Mr. Stone asked me to bring Noelle here. He and Dad had several other things they needed to talk about."

V's phone buzzes, and she takes the phone call. From the looks of it, it's important. She starts walking back and forth.

"Everything okay?" I ask when she plops on the chair.

"No, my brother got his military assignment today. He leaves for Germany tomorrow. If I want to talk to him before he goes, I have to be back at the hotel to skype with him in an hour."

"Okay, let's go." I give her shoulder a squeeze.

Everyone agrees, and we all walk back to the hotel subdued. No one really talks. It feels wrong to talk about anything exciting when V is getting ready to say goodbye to her brother.

We all start to go our separate ways once we hit the hotel lobby. I give V a quick hug, and then she heads off.

"It's too bad she was here when her brother got the call," Noelle says.

"I know." My phone buzzes, stopping me from saying anything else. It's Warren.

Hey, girl. Sorry to do this, but I missed my flight. Rain check on our date?

Of course. What happened?

Semi-truck broke down. Have to take it in.

Oh no. Good luck. :)

Thanks. I'll make it up to you. Promise.

"Warren and I can't catch a break," I complain to Noelle.

She and I are still in the lobby, which means my shadows are still in the lobby with us.

"You know how I feel about Warren, but I am sorry your date got cancelled."

"It's okay. I just didn't want to hang out in the room tonight. The boys will be happy. They won't have to follow me around anymore today."

"Oh, I just had a great idea to get back at the boys." A mischievous look lights up her face.

"What?"

"Did Mrs. Baron say they had to follow you around today?"

"Yes."

"Let's go shopping."

"That's mean." But I grin, secretly loving it.

"We'll let them choose where we eat. I'm not completely without a heart."

She locks her arm with mine and heads toward the boys, sitting in a few of the chairs in the lobby.

"Are you telling them, or am I?"

"I'll do the honors," she volunteers, as we head toward the boys. "Grace and I want to see the mall here."

They both get up.

"I'll get the taxi," Beau says. "But why you want to see a section of grass is beyond me."

"The other kind of mall." I look him straight in the face, waiting for his reaction.

He doesn't disappoint. "Not shopping," Bennett moans. He looks like he'd rather be on the water setter—one of the dirtiest jobs during planting season—instead of going to a mall.

"Don't worry, we'll let you choose where we eat," Noelle says.

"Let's do something else. Be nice ladies," Beau says, opening the cab car door.

"Okay, you boys don't have to go. We'll see you later," Noelle says, hopping into the cab.

I follow her in. They do, too, grumbling the whole time.

Bennett looks at Noelle.

"Your dad asked me to escort you around today, so I will. And, Grace, you know we would never hear the end of it if we didn't go with you."

"Yup, I know. That's why we picked the mall. Payback boys."

"Really, Grace? You already made me have to listen to Rosanne for hours earlier today. I'd say we're even."

"What?" Bennett asks.

So, Beau tells him about it, while Noelle and I laugh uncontrollably beside them until we get a phone call with very bad news from Mrs. Baron.

By the time we make it back to the hotel, she and Mr. Baron have us all packed up and are waiting with a cab for us when we get there.

"How bad is it?" Bennett asks.

"Bad. We'll know more when we get home and see it," Mr. Baron says.

Chapter 11

WE STAND AT THE EDGE of the field, surveying the destruction. The plants are already wilting and starting to brown around the edges. A fourth of Mr. Baron's fields looks like this—or will begin to by tomorrow. The plants are dead too late in the season to even think about replanting them. This section was planted last, so they would have melons to sell in August.

"Are you okay, John?" Mrs. Baron asks.

He pushes the air out through his teeth, "I'm trying to think about Job and reminding myself it could be far worse."

"I'm sorry, John. When we heard the crop duster fly over the fields, we called the company right away. The pilot was supposed to be spraying somewhere else. By the time they got the pilot radioed, he had already taken out this much," Raul says.

"I know it was an accident. I don't blame you," Mr. Baron says.

"The juice bottling project is going to have to carry us through late summer now," Bennett says.

The plan had always been to use watermelons from Melon Ridge Farms.

"Will we have enough melons?" I worry out loud.

"We were going to buy from some of the southern watermelon farmers in the winter. We'll just have to buy from them earlier this year," Mr. Baron says.

He gives the fields one last look and waves us all toward the vehicle. It still has all of our suitcases in it. We basically got off the plane and into the car, so we could head straight to the fields.

"Bennett, Beau, you two see where we are at with the watermelon production. Check the fields to see what they are yielding. Pam, you and Grace get everything ready for juice production. The shed is basically done and waiting on us to start. We'll just have to move the start time up. I'll make some calls about buying melons," he says, pulling the car into the drive.

The boys jump into the old farm truck and head toward the packing shed. Mr. Baron already has the phone to his ear. Mrs. Baron and I head to her office to work on the marketing side of everything. We need flyers and an ad campaign. The bottles will need to be designed, and we still need a name for the juice before anything else can get started.

"Grace, call the bottling company and place the order please. Tell them to go with the first label I faxed over a couple of days ago. See if they can expedite shipping, too."

"Yes, ma'am," I say, picking up the phone.

"The bottles will be here by the end of the week," I tell her.

"Great. Now call the supermarkets that are on your road trip tour and see if they would like to purchase a couple of cases. I have a few bigger chains already lined up, but it makes sense to sell them where you are, too, especially if we give out samples while you're there."

I pick up the phone and start dialing. When I'm done, all the stores I will be visiting want to carry the product.

"Do you want me to call the bigger supermarkets now?" I ask.

"Let's wait. We'll generate some publicity this way first. The bigger chains can sell it after our product release party," she decides.

"Sounds good. Do you want me to order Bo's Pizza for supper?"

"Perfect. The boys will be home soon, and we can all talk while we eat."

"I can't sign that." Surprise at how generous the Barons are being makes my voice raise more than I wanted. I try again. "I don't deserve that much of the profits from the watermelon juice company."

"It was your idea," Mr. Baron points out.

"Just sign it," Beau says.

"What my Neanderthal brother is trying to say is, it was Dad's idea, and Mom loved it. You know what happens when she wants something," Bennett says.

"I usually get my way," Mrs. Baron says with a wink.

"Don't we know it?" I grumble under my breath.

Mr. Baron shakes his head.

"Grace, you've always been a part of our family. We love you. You deserve this. Please sign the contract."

I try to look at it from the business side. I will always have some income, even when I go to college. Mr. Baron knows what he's doing, and he has a lot of connections. He is a good choice for a business partner. I grab the pen.

"Okay, you guys talked me into it. I'll sign." I exhale and take the pen.

Mrs. Baron claps her hands, and the guys seem to relax around the table.

"By the way, what are we going to call this stuff? Watermelon Juice isn't really all that catchy."

"I was thinking Watermelon Nectar. At least that's what I put on the bottles," Mrs. Baron says.

"That's perfect." Excitement makes me sound louder than usual.

"Yeah, great name, Mom," Beau says.

"So, when does production start?" Bennett asks.

"Monday," Mr. Baron replies.

I borrow the old farm truck to head home. The house is dark and empty, since Gramps is still on his mission trip. Gramps and I have been emailing back and forth, so I turn on the laptop, hoping for another email. Then, I lug my suitcase into my room and begin the worst part of the entire traveling process—unpacking. The email icon dings on my screen, showing a message from Gramps. I hurry to start a load of laundry, so I can see what he has to say.

He's having the time of his life. The natives love him. He's getting to share God's Word with kids who have never heard about Him. Gramps attached several pictures of himself with the kids from the orphanage. The kids are all smiles, even though it's apparent they are very poor. The crinkles at Gramps' eyes show he's content in the fact that he's doing what God made him to do.

Some of Gramps' favorite sayings are "Be happy in what you do" and "Know that a person is at their happiest when they are doing what God made them to do." It's what he said to me right before I competed for the Miss Midwest Watermelon Queen title. What's funny is I've been the happiest I've been in a while. Sure, the pain of losing my family is still camped out in my heart, but it's bearable. The Barons have loved me and looked out for me. Even Beau is bearable in small doses. And when I think he's at his most terrible, I try to remind myself that Beau lost someone he loved the night of the accident, too.

I pick up the laptop and head to the sofa. Gramps has missed out on a lot, so I catch him up. I send him a couple pictures of me in Washington, D.C., and I tell him about what happened with Mr. Baron's watermelon fields. I hit send and grab the TV remote. Tomorrow is Sunday and church. I have nothing planned but to relax and watch old, romantic movies.

I wake to the sound of the front screen door opening. I check the clock. It's only 8:00 at night. I must have dozed off on the sofa. The screen door rattles again. Then, nothing. I quickly scramble to the kitchen and grab the first thing I see—Gramps' frying pan. I sneak back to the front door and wait. I feel for my phone in my pocket. Shoot, I left it on the sofa.

The screen door opens. The intruder must have picked the lock. It sounds like he's doing the same thing with the front door now. My eyes are frozen open as the front doorknob turns. A boot steps through. Then, it's a shoulder. I raise the frying pan, close my eyes, and swing. I hit something because my arm jars with the impact, and there's a giant thud.

"Ow! Grace, what in the world—"

That sounded a lot like Beau. I open my eyes to see him rubbing his shoulder and lying on the ground.

"Oh no, Beau, sorry, I thought you were trying to break into the house," I groan, still standing there with the frying pan in my hand.

"No, just needed to get my phone out of the truck."

"Why didn't you just get in the truck and get it?"

"Couldn't. You locked the doors."

"You could have called or knocked."

He gets up and heads to the sofa.

"I did both. Neither worked, so I got worried. The truck was in the driveway, and you weren't answering."

"I was asleep," I holler from the kitchen, while putting an ice pack together.

"I can see that. Anyway, I tried the door a couple of times. When that didn't work, I remembered the hidden key."

I put the ice pack on his shoulder.

"Ah, thank you." He puts his hand on the bag to keep it in place. "How bad is it?"

"I'll live. Lucky for me you never were good at swinging a bat."

"Stop trying to be funny. Should I call your parents?"

"Really, I'm fine. There's a bruise, but you mostly got the side of my arm. No need to call Mom and worry her."

"I'll go get your phone."

I grab the keys off the counter and head out to the truck. I snatch his phone out of the cup holder and head back in. He's in the kitchen, popping popcorn.

"It's where it always is. Hope you don't mind. I'm not really ready to walk back yet."

"Sure, no problem," I say, dropping on the sofa.

"So, what are we watching?" he asks.

I aim the remote at the TV. "Old, romantic movies."

"Come on; be nice. You *did* hit me with a frying pan."

"I *am* nice; besides, you tried to break into my house."

"I have one word for you—frying pan."

"That's two words."

"Doesn't matter. You can't beat that. Now hand over the remote."

He leans over and snatches it out of my hand.

"Hey!" I protest.

He leans away, so I can't reach it.

"You take my popcorn and my TV. Anything else you want?" I grumble.

He doesn't say anything. He just arches his brow and gives me a sideways smirk, reminding me of our conversation by the pond. Heat rushes to my face.

"I didn't mean it like that." I drum my fingers on the armrest of the sofa, trying to ignore the awkward silence.

"Maybe I'd better go after all. Thanks for the popcorn." He raises the bowl.

I follow him to the door.

"Beau, I didn't mean—"

"Don't worry about it. It's getting late, anyway. Mom wanted me to invite you to dinner after church tomorrow."

He keeps cutting me off, so I say what I know he needs to hear, so he can leave.

"Tell her I'll be there. And you should just take the truck now, and then we won't have to take it back tomorrow."

I toss him the keys. He catches them easily and gets into the truck. I watch him drive off, confused about the thoughts he left swirling around inside me.

I slide into my normal pew at church. The green cushion isn't very soft, but it does remind me of Gramps. I find the brown, tattered hymnal and start bookmarking the pages we'll use later in the service. The front of the sanctuary is beautiful with white flowers and burning candelabras. The stained glass windows cast a pink and red glow on the floor.

Several people stop by to ask how Gramps is doing and to check on me. With my schedule lately, I've not been here as regularly as I would have liked. The junior pastor is in the pulpit today. With Gramps gone, he's taken over all the pastoral duties. It feels different to see him there, leading worship.

I glance behind me to see if the Barons have made it yet. They're in their spot. Mrs. Baron is put together like always. The whole family is stunning, really. For one small moment, I let myself believe what Beau has been saying to me, and my insides start to heat up.

Then I feel guilty because there's Warren, and he's been more than I could have imagined. Besides, Beau and I have too much history to ever work. These last couple of days, Warren's been silent, though, not answering my messages or texts. I don't want to be that girl, so

I've laid off leaving messages, but I wonder why he's not returning any of my calls.

The organ music starts, signaling the start of the service, so I face forward and listen to the junior pastor's message.

Chapter 15

I FIND MYSELF IN FRONT of the camera again. This time, I'm shooting for the Watermelon Nectar campaign. Mrs. Baron insisted that I be the face of the campaign because it was my idea. The makeup artist airbrushes me to perfection, while Beau lounges in a chair on set. He's got his earbuds in and the usual disagreeable expression on his face. Mrs. Baron is taking care of last-minute details with the stores I'll be at in a couple of days, so she couldn't be here. Bennett and Mr. Baron are overseeing the start of the juice production today, so Beau is here with me instead.

My fingernails are painted a deep plum color. The stylist put me in a lavender dress that wraps around the waist and hits right above the knees. It will work perfectly for the shoot and will make the coral color of the bottle stand out. Right now, the cameraman is taking snapshots of the bottle on a silver back drop until I'm out of the chair.

The stylist is finally happy with my hair and sends me to the photographer. He wastes no time and starts clicking away on his camera the moment I hit the set. He does pause every once in a while to give a direction. Sometimes, the directions are for me, other times for his assistants.

"Do we have a table?" The photographer asks his assistant.

She scurries off to find one. Another crew member gives me a bottle with a bent, mint green straw coming out of it. A small, silver, round table makes it to the set, complete with matching chair.

"Have a seat, Grace. And pretend you're drinking out of the straw," he instructs, while still looking through the lens of the camera.

I try a few poses, and he snaps a few pictures.

"It just feels awkward," I mumble.

"You're right. We need someone on the other side," he says, looking around the room.

"You there," he points to Beau. "Want to be in a few pictures?"

"No, thanks," Beau says.

He doesn't even bother to take his earbuds out.

If Mrs. Baron wasn't taking care of something else right now, I'm sure she'd have him by the ear, dragging him onto the set herself.

The photographer turns to his assistant and asks, "How long until we can get someone in here? I want to go this direction with the ad."

"An hour or two," comes her disgruntled reply.

"Come on, Beau. Just do it. We'll be done quicker, and then you can get back to the farm." I pressure him with the one thing I know will work.

"Fine," he finally agrees.

That's all the agreement everyone needs. The stylist takes him to her chair, while a crew member runs back and forth with clothing options—first putting them next to Beau and then checking to see how they go with my dress. The photographer continues to direct changes on the set.

"Get rid of the chairs, and put something under the table to make it higher."

The crew rushes around, making the changes. Two bottles with straws are placed on the table. Beau walks onto the set in a white, button-down shirt and khaki pants. They've managed to get rid of his boots and replaced them with oxfords. They've side-parted his hair and swooped it over and up. He looks good. Really good.

"Ready?"

"Let's just get this done," he grumbles, resigned to his fate.

We head to the table and pretend to drink Watermelon Nectar, while the photographer takes pictures from every angle manageable. He steps back and looks at a few on his camera.

"I want one bottle and two straws. Let's see what that looks like," he says.

Our two bottles are replaced with one.

"Okay, you two, we're ready when you are," the photographer says.

Beau and I bend down to pretend-drink from our straws again, which pretty much puts us nose to nose. I've never noticed before, but he smells like pine trees and the outdoors. It's a little bit intoxicating. I look up at Beau.

"Hold that pose," the photographer shouts.

What feels like a million snaps and clicks later, he finally releases us.

"Okay, you two just inspired me. I want to try something new." The photographer starts issuing commands.

The table gets whisked away, and a new drink is placed in my hand.

"Grace, stand there pretending to drink the juice. Beau, do the same thing and hold her hand."

Beau grabs my hand and intertwines his fingers with mine. His hands are rough like sandpaper, but warm, and oddly comforting.

More flash bulbs, and then he says, "Beau, lean down and kiss her on the temple."

It's not romantic. It's awkward because Beau has to stand there like that for what feels like forever, while the photographer tries various angles. He steps back and checks his camera one more time before finally calling a wrap to the shoot. Beau steps back, rubbing his jaw.

"Finally. My face was going numb."

"You poor thing." Sarcasm creeps into my voice. "I'm the one who had your dry, cracked lips on the side of my head."

I resist the urge to wipe off the side of my face like a four-year-old.

"Never had any complaints before."

"Uck, you're such a guy."

"I was just trying to be funny."

"You weren't."

We head our separate ways to get changed back into our normal clothes. I scrub my face clean and get my jeans and t-shirt on. I pull my hair up in a messy bun and slip on my flip flops. I left my rubber boots at the shed.

We meet in the studio, where the crew is running around putting everything back in its place. Beau's back to his work shirt, jeans, and steel-toed boots.

"Thanks." I wave to the photographer, who is already at his computer, working on the ads. He doesn't stop or look up.

"I'll have several of the shots and flyer options sent over by this afternoon," he assures us.

We go through a drive-thru on our way back to the packing shed. I unwrap the paper from Beau's burger and put his fries in the extra cup holder.

"Sorry, no ketchup," I say.

"It's okay." He takes a handful of fries from the carton in the cup holder.

My phone buzzes. It's a text from Warren.

Hi, pretty girl. Sorry I've been in the fields. Can you talk tonight?

I respond back, and we make plans for his call tonight. At least he has a good excuse. If the melons were coming off the vine like they were for us a couple of weeks ago, I understand.

"Who was that?" Beau asks.

"Warren."

"What was his excuse for not calling for a week?"

"It wasn't a week."

"Close enough."

"Not that it's any of your business, but the melons are at full production right now. He was in the fields." I defend Warren, but I am a little disappointed he's not been available lately.

Beau snorts in response. I ignore it, as he drops me off at the packing shed and heads out to the fields. I take over the sorting of the melons from Raul, as other crew members load them into their boxes, then onto the semi-truck.

By midafternoon, we have enough watermelons set aside to take to the converted juice-making barn, so Raul hitches up the wagon to the tractor and heads off. We are going to need that contract with another melon supplier soon. We leave in two days for the supermarket tour, and the commercial for the juice still needs to be shot.

The phone rings from its spot on the post of the packing shed. I hit the kill switch on the melon-washing machine and grab the phone.

"Hello?"

It's Mrs. Baron.

"Grace, perfect. Can you head into the office? We have a couple of contracts to look over for purchasing melons for the juice company. Mr. Baron wants you here to help decide."

I hear the tractor before I see it.

"Raul's almost here. I'll be there in a few minutes," I promise.

I just need to wait until he gets back, so he can take over at the shed again. I have a few crew members set up new boxes and send two to do inventory in the refrigerated shed. Our next shipment isn't due to be packed until tomorrow, so we are ahead of schedule.

Mr. Baron is in the kitchen of the office. He's got paperwork spread out all around him on the worn, oak table. Mrs. Baron puts a mug of coffee down by him and takes a seat.

"We have three contracts to look at," he explains, pointing to each one on the table.

"Can you give me the rundown of each?" I ask, sitting opposite of him.

"Sure. But this first one from the Dixons probably won't work, anyway. They can't promise us the number of melons we will need."

"Okay, who else do we have?"

"The Hartleys have offered a pretty good deal. They are a little more expensive, but they also allow for an extra shipment or two if we need it."

Hearing that Warren's family has made an offer makes my heart speed up a little.

"And the other one?"

"Cheaper by about a cent-and-a-half per pound, but there's no safety net of being able to purchase another load if necessary."

"Who does this one come from?"

"The Masons. They're a smaller farm operation."

"Could we have a backup buyer in place if we took the Mason's deal?"

"Not likely."

"Anything else I need to know?"

"Both are three-year contracts," Mr. Baron says, "and we've decided to let you make the final call. It will be your first decision made as co-owner."

"What if I make a mistake?"

"That's all part of the business," he says gently.

My eyes go round, and I swallow hard. I can feel my heart beat all the way to my feet.

He must have realized the pressure he put on me because he goes on to say, "Honestly, neither choice is bad. We're just leaving it up to you."

"When do we need to know by?"

"Sooner, rather than later. I'd say by the end of next week."

Good, I'll have a little time to think about it during the supermarket tour.

"Are you going to tell me what you think at all?"

"Honestly, both have good spots and both have bad spots. You just have to weigh the good with the bad."

I get up and head to the door. "I will, and I promise to have your answer by Wednesday of next week."

Mr. and Mrs. Baron smile and nod their heads in agreement.

Warren calls, and I force myself not to answer it on the first ring. "Hello."

"Hi, pretty girl."

"So, what have you been up to?"

"It's been crazy over here, and being down a truck for a couple of days really put us behind."

"I bet. D.C. wasn't the same without you."

"Sorry I had to bail on you. I have good news, though."

"Really? What is it?"

"Dad is giving me a couple days to spend with you during your supermarket tour."

"That's awesome! How are you getting there?"

"I'll fly out and meet you at your first Fresh grocery store in Indy."

We soon hang up, and my heart takes a while to slow back down to its normal beat.

Chapter 16

THE BLACK TOUR BUS SITS in front of my house. I try to downplay my excitement, so no one notices. Tomorrow, I'll get to see Warren. I haven't told anyone because I don't want the drama, and besides, they can't tell him not to show up at a public supermarket or maybe all of my promotions I happen to be at tomorrow.

Bennett is loading my overstuffed suitcase under the bus, while Mrs. Baron organizes the camera crew. They will be taping during the actual driving and during the stops at the Fresh grocery store. They have their own van that will carry most of the equipment; but because a cameraman will be with us during the drive, too, there are extra things to work out.

Beau and Mr. Baron are packing the white refrigerated truck with the new Watermelon Nectar juice. The white sides of the truck make the red painted letters of the Melon Ridge Farms sign stand out. The posters and signs arrived yesterday. They aren't the ones from my photo shoot. Those are being saved for the product ad campaign launch party. These are strictly for introducing the brand. They have a large picture of the bottle on a green background. Mrs. Baron also had stickers made with the logo on them.

Mrs. Baron gives Mr. Baron a goodbye kiss, and we all load up in our assigned vehicles. The camera crew—minus the cameraman,

Drew—all pile in to the fifteen-passenger van. There's only four other people in the van, but most of the space is taken up by camera equipment. Bennett and Beau climb into the refrigerated truck and make the end of our little caravan.

Drew stands to the side of the tour bus, getting it all on camera. He gives Mrs. Baron and me the thumbs up to go ahead and climb onboard the bus. Vinnie, our Latino bus driver, shuts the door and starts rolling. He only goes about fifty feet, then stops. We wait for Drew to catch up and climb inside, so we can really begin the trip.

"We'll have several starts and stops like these during the trip," Drew says.

Mrs. Baron and I nod our heads.

"This one was great, though. We only needed one take."

He leans back against the sofa opposite of ours, looking around the bus. He looks like a rock star, resting on his tour bus after a long performance.

"It's not bad," Drew says, talking about the interior.

It's all browns and blacks on the inside, and it definitely has the feel of a tour bus that's been used for some celebrities. Two brown, leather sofas are bolted to the floor, one on either side of the walkway. There's a small kitchenette with a sink and refrigerator. The back of the bus has a small bedroom on each side with bunk beds protruding from the wall. The very back has the bathroom and another sitting area. For better or worse, it's home for the next ten days.

I find a seat on the sofa, then ask Mrs. Baron, "What is our schedule when we hit Indy?"

"You have two stores this afternoon, right before we reach Indianapolis. Then three more the next day in Indy."

"Okay." I nod, then lean back to enjoy the ride.

I want to talk with Mrs. Baron about the contracts for the watermelons, but I don't feel comfortable doing that in front of the camera, so I pull up the website that was created for this tour. I click on Noelle's little dot on the map and a picture of her pops up with a blurb about where she's headed.

"That's cool."

"What?" Drew asks.

"The site they made of the Fresh grocery store tour." I show him my computer screen.

Curious, I do the same thing for me. My picture and blurb talk about Terre Haute, Indiana. The dots and blurbs change as we move from one location to another. At night, each camera crew will edit the tape from the day and upload it under their assigned queen's tab on the site.

Our first stop is only an hour away, so we roll into the Fresh grocery store parking lot and have some time to spare. Drew hops out first to video us stepping off the bus. Mrs. Baron and I go find the box that is under the bus that has all of our promotional supplies. Bennett helps me carry that in, while Mrs. Baron meets with the store manager, and they plan where to set the display. Beau carries the crate of juice samples in with us.

Drew continues to follow us with the camera. And now that we're going into the store, another cameraman follows us around, too. We stop in front of the produce section, where the watermelons are being displayed. Some are in a bin like the ones we use in the packing shed. Other watermelons have been cut in half and are plastic-wrapped, ready to be sold. They've left a section bare for the

Watermelon Nectar, so Beau starts stocking the refrigerated shelves. He's careful to make sure the brand name is shown on all the labels.

Bennett begins the setup of our posters and banners. The large Watermelon Nectar posters hang on either side of the table that the store manager had put up. I cover it with a white tablecloth and begin cutting the melon into bite-sized pieces. When I'm done, Bennett has me help him hang our association's banner across the front of the table. Mrs. Baron puts flyers out about the health benefits of the watermelon, and then she organizes the samples of watermelon and juice.

I take my crown out of my case. It never gets old watching the stones reflect specks of light. I put it on, then my sash. I'm in a black shorts jumpsuit with scalloped edges on the shorts. My red chunky necklace has several strands that are clasped together on the side with a giant, sparkly watermelon broach. Black heels complete the look.

Mrs. Baron and I take the front table while the boys work at cutting and refilling watermelon samples when our first customer comes up to the table. It's a mom and a little girl.

"Hi, would you like to try a sample?" I hold up a small cup with the juice in it and smile.

The little girl nods. I look to her mother before handing them each a sample of the watermelon and juice.

"This is amazing," the woman says about the juice.

"Thanks. I'm happy you like it." I can't help but feel a little pride in our product.

Then, like they taught us at the workshop, I ask, "Would you like me to help you pick a ripe watermelon out of the bunch?"

"That would be great," she agrees.

So, I go over how it should be heavy for its size and make a hollow sound when you thump it and that its underbelly should be yellow.

"Momma, I want the juice," the little girl says.

"Here you go, ma'am," Beau says, handing the woman a bottle.

The little girl claps her hands, excited about the treat.

I turn to the little girl. "Would you like a sticker?" I grab the roll off the table and offer her a couple.

She reaches out for one, but I decide to hand her two. "There you go. Now you have one for later," I say.

The little girl takes them and waves as her mom pushes the cart on by.

"First sale of the day." I clap my hands together, feeling successful.

"We're going to stop rolling and head to the van for a bit," Drew says. He and the other cameraman take their cameras off their shoulders.

"I think you guys got a lot of good stuff already, anyway," Mrs. Baron says.

A steady stream of customers files through the produce section of the store. Bennett keeps us stocked on samples, while Beau continues to refill the juice shelves. My roll of stickers is almost gone, and we've been out of juice for an hour when it's time to close the booth down.

"How'd we do on the watermelons?" Mrs. Baron asks.

One of the perks of a store allowing us to promote in-store is that most of their stock is sold, so they make a lot of money. Even the juice we're selling is product they purchased from us, so it looks really good that it's moving so fast. We were barely able to keep it on the shelves.

"Only a half a bin left," Bennett says.

We quickly work to put everything back into their boxes, and the boys start loading it back into the tour bus. Mrs. Baron and I search out the store manager, thanking her for letting us be in her store.

The boys and crew are waiting for us in the parking lot. There's just enough time to eat something quickly before we head to the other side of town to do another promotion. We agree to grab food from a drive-thru, so we aren't so rushed and have enough time to set up.

We pull up to the next Fresh supermarket and begin the process of setting up all over again. This time, it goes even faster because we were able to work the kinks out from the first store. The manager greets us as our camera crew tapes my every move. The juice flies off the shelves, and Beau has trouble keeping it restocked. We've gone through a third of the truck, and we haven't even finished our second stop on the tour. Mrs. Baron leaves me to man the booth and heads to the bus to make a phone call back to the farm about sending more product. It will have to be shipped to some of our other stops that are further down the line.

Bennett continues to slice the melon into bite-sized samples, while I hand them out. We've really gone through the bins of melons in this store. Beau has given up on keeping the shelves stocked. He just has one row up and then pulls the juice out of the box to give to the customers.

The manager stops by with a news crew from the local area. The anchorman stands in front of us as we continue to pass out samples and talk to customers.

"This is Mark Abernathy from Channel 7 News, coming to you live at the Fresh supermarket. As you can see behind me, the Midwest Watermelon Queen is busily passing out watermelon samples grown from watermelon farmers right here in our own state."

He pauses for a moment and then answers a question he got from his earpiece. Then, the camera light goes off and he starts walking over to our table.

"I'd like to ask you a couple of questions, if that's ok."

"Sure, no problem," I answer him back.

Luckily, the main stream of customers has dwindled to a slow trickle. The boys will be able to handle it, while I answer a few questions. It's a little weird that Mrs. Baron isn't back from the bus yet. I don't really have time to wonder about it anymore than that because he starts asking me questions. He wants to know what I do and what all the watermelon has to offer its customers. I'm able to answer easily, thanks to the training week we had in Atlanta.

Then he switches to more personal questions.

"So, who are these two guys working with you today?" he asks.

"Bennett and Beau Baron," I point to each one as I say his name. "They are part of Melon Ridge Farms, a farm about sixty miles south of here." I try to keep it short and sweet.

"And how did they get the opportunity to work with such a beautiful young lady as yourself?"

"Oh, I've known the Baron boys from the time I was a little girl. They're more like family than anything else."

"Nice. So, it's a family affair," he suggests. "From what I understand, you guys have developed a new watermelon juice drink. Care to tell me a little about it?"

"I'd love to. It's all the yummy goodness of a watermelon, but in a drink. It's easy to take with you and refreshing any time of the year."

Beau brings me a container of the Watermelon Nectar to hand the newscaster. He takes it and gives it a try on camera.

"That *is* good." He takes another drink from the bottle.

"It's coming soon, so look for it in stores near you," I tell them before the cameraman stops recording.

"That was great back there."

"Thanks."

"It will be on the news tonight around eight." He offers his hand for a handshake.

Bennett joins me and Beau and offers his hand, too.

"Thanks again for the news coverage," he says.

"My pleasure," Mark says.

He and his cameraman quickly pack up and head out.

It's actually time for us to start cleaning up, too. We've run out of watermelons to sell, and we have to save some juice because the next shipment won't be ready for a couple of days. The boys work on tearing everything down, while I box up the flyers, stickers, and tablecloths. It doesn't take long before we're done. Drew puts his camera away, too. I had totally forgotten he was even there.

"I got footage of the news crew taping you. I think it will look really cool on the video blurb."

"Awesome. I can't wait to see it." I am pleased that he got good footage, but I'm tired, too. It's a lot to always be on for the camera.

"Then I better get on it." He heads to the van to start working on editing.

The boys and I take our load to the bus, where Mrs. Baron is waiting.

"They sent over the flyers for the product launch party. I love them."

"Can we see them?" I ask.

"I'll show you in a minute. Let's get this bus on the move."

She ushers us in and continues to talk. "I've been able to talk with the ad campaign manager, and she's got the storyboards done for the shoot. We're actually going to shoot it tonight."

"Sounds good," I manage to get out, but really, I'm tired. I've been on my feet in heels all day.

"Bennett, you'll need to drive the refrigerated truck. I need Beau here to see the storyboards."

"Why?" Beau asks.

"Good luck, little brother," Bennett says, laughing on his way out of the bus.

"The ad they chose to go with is this one," Mrs. Bennett says, pulling up the image of me and Beau holding hands and drinking the juice. At the top of the poster, it says WATERMELON NECTAR. Then, underneath us in a scripted font, it says, *Make Life Sweeter.*

It looks really good. I try to find something to say about it that doesn't reference me and Beau as a couple. All I can come up with is, "Nice."

"Yes, I'm pleased with it. You two make a cute couple—"

"Mom," Beau interrupts.

"I'm just stating what I see in print; you chose to take it to a personal level," Mrs. Baron says.

Trying to change the subject, I ask, "So what about the storyboards?"

"Yes, we have about a half an hour before we get to the studio. I need you two to understand your parts. You both will be front and center for the ad campaign."

Beau groans. I do, too, only it's on the inside because working with Beau sounds about as much fun as turning vines in an entire field by myself. Terrible and laborious.

Chapter 17

ON THE OUTSIDE, THE STUDIO doesn't look like much more than a pole barn, but the interior more than makes up for the outside. They will do our makeup first. Then they'll figure out what outfits to put us in. Beau and I are going to be shooting three to four different commercials tonight. So, while everyone else is on the bus sleeping, we're here working. Mrs. Baron is with us, too. She always has her finger on the pulse of everything to do with the ad campaign.

Dressed in a white, strapless ball gown and brown cowboy boots, I walk to the large green screen at the back of the studio. Someone has been working all day to make the floor look like a planted watermelon field. They have the vines and large, ripe watermelons set in rows. Even soil was trucked in and spread around to create a fake melon patch. They've put grass around the edges, and I'm told the green screen will do the rest.

For the first scene, I'm supposed to run down the rows with the front of my dress pulled up so that it flows out when I move. Beau stands on the side with his arms crossed, waiting. First, I run toward the camera. Then, they have me run toward the green screen. They want me to look over my shoulder every so often, too. They play soft music in the background to create a romantic atmosphere. I'm supposed to look carefree and in love. Those were the director's notes I read before taking the set. I run forward and backward a total of nine times before the director is happy with what I've done.

"Add the boy," the director says. He's an older man in his late-forties, with a balding comb-over that he hides with a sock hat and beard.

Beau shuffles his feet but meets me in our fake field. We follow the storyboards, which are small, drawn pictures that show us what each frame of the video will look like when they're done taping us. Beau grabs my hand, and we run toward the green screen and then back to the camera. Just like what they showed us on the bus. The director isn't happy with how we did it, so we do it again, then again, until he does like it.

"It seems like all I ever do is run with you," Beau says, as we set up for another take of us running toward the green screen.

"At least this time, we aren't in the rain."

"Yes, this is definitely better. We're together in a fake field, and they plan to use me in a national commercial." Sarcasm drips from his voice.

"I'm sorry being with me is such a burden." I cross my arms and look away.

"Why do you do that?"

"I'm not doing anything."

"Yes, you are."

The director yells action, and we take off running again—which, thankfully, cuts off the conversation.

"Stop running," Beau says, easily keeping up with me.

"I can't. We're shooting a commercial where we're supposed to run."

The director yells cut right before we reach the green screen. I'm breathing a little heavy, but I turn to look up at Beau.

"That's not what I meant, and you know it."

He walks off set, leaving me standing there in the middle of my fake watermelon field, ball gown and all, feeling pierced to the bone. If Beau had wanted to hurt me, then his words hit their mark, leaving me with some soul-searching to do.

I head off in the opposite direction to wait until I'm called back to set. I check my phone. No new messages. Warren had texted when he was getting on the plane, but I've heard nothing since. He's probably trying to get set up in his hotel room.

In the next scene, Beau and I are supposed to intertwine our hands and lean forward, so our foreheads touch. Then we pull back and drink the juice.

"Beau, smile at her," the director says.

Beau looks down at me, a smile on his face, and for one small second, my stomach flops. Why had I never noticed what a great smile he has?

"Grace, you look afraid. Smile back."

More coaching from the director has me plastering on a smile.

"C'mon, guys, sell the romance. We need it for the ad campaign," the director says, coaching us through the exchange.

We finish three bottles before the director has what he wants. We drop hands and step back from one another. My stomach rolls with three bottles worth of juice in it.

"I know I shouldn't say this, but I'm starting to not like watermelon juice," Beau grimaces and rubs his hand over his stomach.

"I feel it sloshing around, too." I press my lips together to try not to think about the amount of juice I've consumed today.

We walk back to our chairs and wait. They always re-fluff the fake vines and add more dirt between takes.

"Beau, what you said earlier about me not running. I just want you to know I'm getting there. Warren has helped me."

Beau starts to say something, but I cut him off.

"Your family has helped me, too. I couldn't have done it without you all."

I tear up a little. Thinking about it brings the fact that Gramps isn't a phone call away anymore, and sometimes an email doesn't cut it.

"I made you cry," Beau says.

"No, it's not that. I miss Gramps is all."

He gives me a wrinkled napkin.

"Sorry, it's all I had." There's a little laugh in his voice.

I take it.

"Thanks."

I dab the corners of my eyes to keep from ruining an hour's worth of makeup application.

"Can I ask you a question?"

"Shoot."

"What made you stop running? I've noticed a certain change in you." Then, playfully, I add, "I mean, you're still grumpy, but you're not all bad. I guess." I nudge him a little with my shoulder.

"Thanks. I think." He's smiling, so I know he gets my joke.

Then he gets serious.

"It was when we were eating pizza in D.C.—you know, the conversation about the accident. I was telling you to let go and live, but I wasn't doing that. I was holding on, too."

I nod and force a hard swallow back down my throat.

"Anyway, I decided to give it all to God, so I prayed it all over to Him, and then I tried to explain it to you in the truck, but you ran away from me before I could get it all out." He finishes with a small, sideways grin that makes my stomach flop even more than the last time.

"I did not run." I sound more defensive than I want to, but there's nothing I can do about it at this point.

"I had to hold your car door open, so you wouldn't close it and drive off on me."

"Fine. Maybe I did run a little, but you dumped a lot on me during that truck drive. It was a lot to process."

"You're right. I shouldn't have unloaded it all on you like that."

He rubs the back of his neck with his hand, which I'm quickly learning is his signature move when he feels frustrated or guilty.

"Truce?" Beau asks, offering his hand.

"Truce," I agree, putting my hand in his.

We walk toward the snack table and grab some coffee.

"Beau?"

"Yeah?"

"So, this may sound weird, but I'm happy I'm shooting this commercial with you."

"Really? Why?"

"Yeah, at least I know you. It would have been awkward doing some of the poses and romance stuff with some stranger I had never met. I definitely wouldn't have felt as safe."

"This," he motions his arm out to point at the camera and the set, "is not my idea of fun; but if it made it easier for you, I'm glad I could help."

The director calls us back to the set to finish the taping. This time, I'm supposed to run toward Beau, and he's going to lift me up by the waist, then twirl me around in a circle. My arms are supposed to be on his shoulders.

The director yells, "Action!" I take off toward Beau, who is standing in the middle of our fake field. He grabs me by the hips and lifts, but I didn't jump high enough or something because I crash straight into him and somehow elbow him in the jaw, while my boot connects with his shin. He manages not to fall backward or drop me on the ground, but my landing is more of a stumbling mess as I trip over watermelons in the row. The only thing that keeps me from landing in a heap of tulle and fabric is Beau's hand around my elbow.

"You're dangerous. If we hadn't just called a truce, I'd think you were trying to get even," Beau says, rubbing his jaw with his free hand.

"I'm sorry. Are you okay?"

He still has his arm around my elbow. I shake my arm, reminding him to let go.

We reset and try it again. This time, it works, and Beau is able to twirl me around in a circle. The director gives us notes after every take. Sometimes, he wants us to smile at each other. Other times, Beau is supposed to set me down, and we are to stare into each other's eyes. During one take, the director yells for Beau to pick me up and carry me in front of him as he walks towards the green screen. We have to do that several more times before the director gets the angle he wants.

When we are given another break while they do damage control on the set, I check my phone. There's a message from Warren, telling me he can't wait to see me. I don't send one back because it's two in the morning, and I'd hate to wake him up. It's funny, but until now, I didn't realize it was so late. The only good news about the late night is that when I wake up in the morning, Warren will be there.

"This is the last one," the director says, calling us back.

Beau and I stand in front of the camera, waiting for instructions.

"Throw her over your shoulders like a sack of potatoes," the director says.

Beau complies, and his shoulder digs into my gut.

"Oof, precious cargo here," I remind him, as he bounces me around a little, trying to get a good hold.

"Sorry, this dress is as big as you are and hard to control." He pushes the tulle out of his face.

"Good. Now, Beau, face the green screen; we're going to have you walk toward it while Grace drinks from the bottle."

The director places Beau and me where he wants us. He has Beau put his spare hand in his pocket. I'm supposed to try to support myself with one forearm while drinking the juice.

"Remember to look happy, Grace. Right now, you look like you're in pain," the director says.

I *am* in pain. Beau's shoulder continues to dig into me, but I smile, trying to look dreamy and in love as I take pretend sips of juice from the Watermelon Nectar bottle.

It's three in the morning when the director finally calls a halt to the taping. Mrs. Baron gets up from her chair, blinking heavily. She walks over to the director to talk about deadlines for the commercial. Beau and I take that as our cue to get out of our costumes. The change into my normal clothes reminds me of how tired I am.

I scrub my face in my changing room, but even after the third wash, there's still eyeliner at the edge of my eyes and lipstick staining my lips. I am too lazy to do anything to my hair, so I just let it fall down in the soft waves created for the commercial. Mrs. Baron and Beau are waiting by the door for me. I shuffle my tired feet toward them and the bus. All I want to do is sleep right now, so that I can spend every second with Warren tomorrow.

I fall onto my bunk bed and fall asleep just as the tour bus pulls out. When I wake up tomorrow, we'll be in Indy, and two more supermarkets will be waiting for me.

The alarm goes off, jarring me awake way before I'm ready. I punch the code into my phone, so I can get to the snooze button to turn it off. I have an hour before the start of my next promotion, so I grudgingly throw my covers off and start getting ready. Most of the crew are probably up and moving around, getting everything set up in the Fresh supermarket. The least I can do is get myself presentable and do my job.

One look in the mirror tells me I'm going to need a lot of dark circle coverage under my eyes. I add an extra layer and some powder. My hair actually looks pretty good from last night's shoot, so I add a curl here and there as needed. Mrs. Baron has my outfit out and waiting. It's a red skirt with pleats and a white lace trim. A white blouse with red cuffs hangs beside black wedges and black sparkly earrings and bangles.

I quickly get dressed and grab some coffee on the way out of the bus. Mrs. Baron and the rest of the crew, minus Beau, are working to carry all the stuff in for the display. Beau's probably sleeping. Honestly, he earned it. The only thing that keeps me going this morning is the fact that Warren will be here today.

"Grace, good morning," Mrs. Baron says when she sees me coming off the bus. "You don't look any worse for the wear."

"Good morning, ma'am," I greet her, but my eyes are already searching for Warren.

"Someone special is here for you, but I put him to work. With Beau sleeping, we need all the help we can get," Mrs. Baron says.

She moves to the side, so I can see Warren carrying in boxes of the juice. I give him a wave and head in his direction.

"Hi," I say.

"Hey, you. I told Mrs. Baron to put me to work. I'm a free man for a couple of days."

Warren puts the box down by the refrigerated shelves and opens his arms for a hug. I go straight into them.

"I missed you," I murmur.

"Missed you too, pretty girl."

We break apart to the sound of clearing throats, but no one really seems to mind. Warren is doing the juice for us today, anyway.

It's the same routine as the other promotions. Watermelon samples and stickers are handed out to customers as we push the sales of the watermelons. My juice flies off the shelves, and Warren has to take several trips to the truck to get more boxes of it.

Drew and his crew tape the people talking to me. At one point, I dangle over the edge of a bin to get a ripe melon out for the customer, and Drew is right there, taping the whole thing.

"That's going to be great for the website," he says.

"I do what I can." I give him a wink, and then I turn to the customer. "Here you go. This one is good and ripe. It will be perfect for grilling."

"Grilling?" The customer asks.

"Here, take a flyer. It tells you what to do. Drizzle it with a bit of balsamic vinaigrette, and you can't go wrong." I put the melon in his cart and hand him a flyer as he heads off to do more shopping.

"We're down to one crate left of juice in the truck. Want me to save it or bring it out?" Warren asks.

"The truck should be delivering the other juice to our other stores this morning. Go ahead and bring it out to sell," Mrs. Baron says.

Warren heads out to the truck, and Bennett continues to cut samples. Customers come and go. Most leave with a Watermelon Nectar bottle or watermelon in their cart.

Chapter 8

AFTER OUR LAST PROMOTION OF the day, we were able to send the refrigerated truck back to the farm with Ace and Tim. One took the semi, while the other drove the truck back. From here on out, the juice will be delivered to the stores before we even get there. Hopefully, they'll even have it stocked, so we don't have to do it.

The moon shines in the bus window, reminding me of my late night yesterday. Mrs. Baron invited Warren to ride with us. Luckily, he took a cab from the airport, so there's no worry about his vehicle. His small, travel suitcase just got shoved under the bus with everything else.

Warren and I sit on a sofa, watching some action movie that just happened to be left on the bus from the last occupants. We can't really talk because everyone is crammed into the front section of the bus. Beau slouches on the other sofa, scrolling through messages or something on his phone. Bennett has a soil magazine that he's zoned in on. He even takes notes on the sides of the paper. Vinnie, our bus driver, has soft jazz music playing quietly through the speaker system on the bus. The only people who aren't here with us are Mrs. Baron and Drew. She went to sleep the moment the bus started rolling, the long hours of the night before catching up to her. Drew's in the van behind us, busy working on uploading the video files from today's promotions.

After about two hours of driving, Vinnie pulls the bus into a gas station.

"There's Chinese takeout over there." Vinnie points in the general direction of the small strip mall. "You guys may want to get that. I don't think we'll see anything else for a while."

He climbs out of his seat and begins filling the bus with gas.

"You want something to eat?" Warren asks me.

"Yeah, sounds good.

We walk hand-in-hand to the restaurant, blissfully alone. For whatever reason, the boys didn't get up to follow us.

"So, anything new happening with you?" he asks.

"Not really. I just did a commercial shoot with Beau, and Mr. Baron is letting me decide who gets the contract to supply watermelons for the juice."

"Really?"

"Yup, and he won't help me out with the decision."

"Maybe I can help."

"You know it's between your farm and someone else's, right?"

"I do. I would be lying if I said we didn't want the contract. But you're more important to me, so if I can help you, then that's what I want to do."

He smiles at me, then looks at his phone.

"Sorry, I have to take this. Will you start to order for us?"

"Sure."

He stays outside, while I head in. Bright lanterns in all different colors hang from the ceiling. Marble statues of Koi fish stand on either side of the entrance. No one is in line, so I walk straight to the counter and order several different things, not knowing what everyone will want. Boxes of crab rangoon, fried dumplings, chicken fried rice, lo mein noodles, and sweet and sour chicken start to pile on top of the counter. I swipe the company credit card and grab the three bags of take out from the counter. I use my elbow to open the door. Warren sees me and disconnects from his call.

"Here, let me help," he offers.

I hand him a couple of the bags, and we walk back to the tour bus.

"Everything okay?"

"Yeah, just my dad checking in on me."

"Did you tell him we made you work on your days off?"

"It's never work when I'm with you."

I smile up at him.

"It was nice having you with us. I don't want you to go back to Texas."

"Well, before I do, I'd be happy to be a sounding board for you with those contracts."

I let out a breath.

"One is cheaper but can't promise extra melons if needed. The other one, from your family, is a little more expensive, but we have the safety net of more watermelons if we need them."

"How is the juice doing so far?"

"You know from today, it's flying off the shelves. I'm sure we'll need the extra melons."

"Sounds to me you already know what to do."

"Anyway your family could match the lower price?"

"I don't think so. We're taking a risk not selling a load and just keeping it in reserve for you."

He's right. It's not fair to ask for the lower price.

"Okay, let's sign the contract when we get back to the bus," I tell him.

"You know it's what I want. I'm happy you agree." He bumps into me on purpose and looks pleased.

"We'll get to spend more time together," I add.

He doesn't respond. He's typing on his phone again.

"Are you sure everything's okay?"

He usually doesn't have his phone out when we're together. Maybe he's getting more comfortable with us as a couple. I never thought I'd get jealous of an electronic device.

"Sorry, yeah, I'm fine. Just some farm stuff. No big deal."

He puts the phone in his pocket as Vinnie opens the bus door. Warren steps to the side and follows me up the steps. Beau and Bennett are where we left them. Vinnie is in the driver's seat, eating one of those gas station burritos and an extra-large big sip drink.

"We have the food," Warren announces to no one in particular.

The boys perk up at the mention of food, following us to the little kitchenette table. Warren puts the bags on the counter, then grabs mine and does the same thing.

"You three get everything out. I'll be back," I throw over my shoulder, but they barely nod in acknowledgment.

I head down the hallway of the bus to the back office area and grab the file folder with the two contracts in it. Mr. Baron has already signed both so that whichever one I choose, I can sign it and then hand it over to the other person to sign. Then, we'll be done. I scrawl my signature across the line.

"You guys better not eat all of the dumplings," I warn, as I walk down the hallway.

The guys are all hovering around the table. They stick their chopsticks into various boxes in rapid succession. I'm not even sure they're chewing the food before they swallow.

"I have the contract for you, Warren. I've already signed it." I place it on the table with a flourish.

Beau looks at the contract, then me. "Grace, can I talk to you for a second?"

He doesn't give me a chance to reply; he has me and the contract in his hands and down the hall in record time.

"Are you sure you want this?" he growls, waving the contract.

But I know what he really means. He doesn't want me choosing Warren's contract just because it's Warren's contract.

"It's the best offer."

"But you'll have to spend more time with him." His voice takes on a hard edge.

"I'm okay with that. It's you who has the problem, remember?" I blast him with my eyes.

I leave Beau standing there with a frown on his face and walk back to Warren, who is waiting happily with a pen.

"Here ya go." I point to where he needs to sign it.

He takes the contract and writes his name quickly. Then, he offers me his hand for a handshake.

"Put 'er there, partner," he says with a wink.

I take his hand, shaking it. "I like the sound of that."

"Me, too."

"I'm going to fax a copy to Mr. Baron and your dad right now," I tell him.

I swipe the box of dumplings and bring it with me. The boys are smart enough to keep their mouths closed about it, but Beau is still standing where I left him, arms folded and his normal scowl in place.

I fire the fax machine up in our little converted office space in the back of the bus. I hit the buttons to send it through and wait for the machine to do its thing. I pull my chopsticks out of my back pocket and dive into the dumplings, hungrier than I realized.

When I make it back to the front of the bus, Beau is back at the table, and the guys have finished off what was left of the food and fortune cookies. They've managed to find their original spots on the sofa and are glued to the baseball game playing on the TV. I bite the inside of my mouth, disappointed. The fortune cookie is my favorite part. Luke and I had a thing where we'd open each other's and read it out loud in an ominous or spooky voice.

Trying to not think about the fortune cookies, I suggest playing a game.

Warren looks at me. "Did you get the contracts faxed?"

"Yep. Now help me talk these boys into a game of cards."

I bat my eyelashes, pretending to flirt with him.

"Yes, ma'am. You guys heard her."

We spread around the table, and I deal. Bennett is his usual good-natured self. Beau is still distant with Warren, but he doesn't say anything embarrassing or act like a jerk. He does keep sending me looks that say he blames me for everything, though. So, I try not to look his direction any more than I have to while playing. After a couple of games, my eyes start closing from the long night before.

"Sorry, guys, I can't keep my eyes open."

The guys throw down their cards on the table, and Warren starts packing them back up.

"I'm beat, too," says Bennett.

He gets up and heads for his and Beau's room with bunk beds.

"Will you be okay on the sofa?" I ask Warren.

"Sure, the sofa's great. I might even stay up and watch a little more TV."

He picks up his phone, checking it again. He's been on it all night. I'm starting to worry about his family, but I don't want to pry, especially since he's said everything is fine several times.

"Okay, well, good night, then," I say.

"Good night," he says, never taking his eyes off his phone.

I start what is becoming a very well-known path down the corridor to my and Mrs. Baron's room.

"Grace, wait," Beau says, stopping me before I can make it to my room.

I turn around and wait for him to catch up.

"I have something for you. I know how you like fortune cookies."

His eyes look conflicted, like he's still angry about the contract and Warren, but vulnerable in a way, too. He reaches into the pocket of his shirt and pulls one out, then places it in my hand.

"How'd you know?"

"Luke." He pauses for a minute, almost like he's trying to decide if he should say more. "He would never eat his when we would eat Chinese. One night, I asked him why he was always grabbing an extra cookie but never eating it. He told me about your tradition."

"He did?" I whisper.

Beau pulls out another cookie, and my mouth goes dry.

"I was wondering if maybe you'd like to read my fortune to me."

"I don't know if I can—"

"It's okay. I can read them for us. I'll read yours first."

I let out a slow breath and hold out my cookie. Fear and the need for this tradition to still be alive twist and jumble around inside my chest. He takes the cookie and cracks it open.

I hold my breath.

"It says, 'Kiss the person across from you.'"

My eyes dart up.

"It does not," I gasp, grabbing at the piece of paper.

He holds it up out of my reach.

"You're right, it doesn't. I just wanted to get rid of some of the tension on your face."

"Congratulations." I roll my eyes, fighting the red that's creeping into my cheeks. "Now tell me what it really says. And don't forget the scary voice this time."

"Okay, it really says: 'Beee mischeeevious, and you weeel not beee loooonesome." He does his best ghost impersonation.

He hands me the slip of paper, and I reread it. Sure enough, it reads, "Be mischievous, and you will not be lonesome."

"I think that should have been your fortune. You're the mischievous one."

"Sorry, it doesn't work that way."

"I think I'll read yours after all." I hold out my hand waiting for him to hand over the cookie."

"I don't know if I should trust you," he hedges, but he places his cookie in my outstretched palm anyway.

I arch an eyebrow and crack open the cookie. I slowly roll out the sheet of paper, trying to make him wonder. Two can play his game, but then I read it and swallow hard.

"Well?"

"Give me a minute. I'm trying to figure out how to say it all spookily," I say, trying to buy some time.

He leans back against his and Bennett's closed door.

"Fame, fortune, and romance are headed your way," I start out, using my ghostly voice. But somewhere around the word *romance*, I taper off into a whisper, and a huge blush that I'm no longer able to fight spreads across my face.

Beau doesn't say anything other than, "Interesting."

I can't look up for some reason, and I get all awkward.

"Um, yeah, so there's your fortune. I got to go now. Good night," I blurt out, finally looking up.

He's just standing there, the corners of his mouth turned up, watching me squirm.

"So, I got to say, I never thought you would get so squeamish on me," he scoffs.

"Hey, no fair. That was hard for me. This is the first time I've read fortunes with someone after the accident."

"You're right. I'm sorry. Forgiven?"

I'm able to smile a little.

"I suppose so."

"Thanks."

We both turn toward our doors, ready for sleep; but before I can close my door behind me, I decide to say more.

"Beau?"

"Yeah?"

He half-turns around.

"Thanks for saving me a cookie."

"Any time."

I close my door behind me. Resisting the urge to over-analyze tonight's events with Warren and his phone and Beau with the cookies, I get ready for bed. Tomorrow will be here with more promotions and media. We both need our rest.

When I wake up in the morning, the bus is empty, except for Vinnie, who is asleep on one of the front sofas of the bus. I quickly put myself together. We have several more hours before our first promotion. I thought everyone would still be having breakfast on the bus, so I peek out the window to see where everyone is. Warren is pulling out his suitcase from under the bus, and a taxi cab is waiting on him.

I throw on shoes and hurry past Vinnie and down the steps of the bus. I walk straight toward Warren, hoping for answers. He sees me coming and says, "Good. I'm happy I got to see you before I left. Dad called this morning; my vacation's over. He needs me back at work."

"Everything okay?"

He seems in a rush, but he stops to talk, while the cab driver puts his luggage in the trunk.

"Just a family thing. But I've got to go. Don't want to miss my flight."

"Of course. Text me when you can."

"Will do, pretty girl. Goodbye."

With that, he jumps into the cab without as much as a backward glance or hug goodbye. I cross my arms and rub my hands over my shoulders, just standing there.

"You okay?" Bennett asks, walking up beside me.

I look around. Everyone but he and Beau have gone back to eating their breakfast. Beau is leaning against the bus, watching me.

"I'm fine."

"Good. For a minute there, I thought I was going to have to try to cheer you up with food. Now all the bacon can be mine."

It's just like Bennett to try to cheer me up. I play along, trying to get over my disappointment of Warren leaving.

"I don't think so," I yell before taking off toward the bus door.

Bennett easily passes me, but Beau waits for me at the door. I pull up short of the doors when his arm shoots out to block me.

"Don't worry. I saved you some."

"Why are you being so nice to me?"

"I want you to be happy, and I told Luke—"

"Don't you dare hide behind that anymore. If I can't run, then you can't hide."

Beau's constant use of Luke as a reason for his behavior ticks me off. I cross my arms over my chest and shift my weight. He stands up tall and shoves his hands in his pockets.

"What do you want me to say?"

"I don't know! Just point me in the direction of the bacon, okay?"

Beau starts chuckling.

"What?"

"Our fight ends with you demanding bacon. It's funny."

"I didn't realize we were fighting."

"Sorry. You just know what to say to make me angry. Can we call a truce again?"

"Yes. I'd rather not fight with you. But so we're clear, I find you to be a grumpy, old bear this morning."

"Did you really just call me a grumpy, old bear?" He rakes his hand through his hair.

"Yup, deal with it." I don't look up as I climb the bus steps.

"I am, but I'm trying to figure out when we resorted to name-calling that a five-year-old would use."

"I thought it was appropriate. Your hair is messy, and your face is still scruffy because you haven't shaved yet this morning. The grumpy part seems to be your normal MO."

I wink at him, so he knows I'm teasing him. Then I walk to the kitchenette table and snag a couple pieces of bacon before I head to my room to get ready. Beau stands where I left him, an amused look on his face.

I look out the window and watch the trees pass by. We've finished our last promotion today and have several hours on the road before our next one. I look back down at my laptop again. The email from Gramps talks about the villagers and the new water well they've been working on. The picture he sends is a close-up. His eyes crease in a smile, while orange, purple, and pink streak across the sky in the background. He looks happy—the happiest I can remember seeing him since before Grandma died.

I let out a sigh and work on my email for him.

I tell him all about the tour and that we've fallen into a pattern with the remaining promotions on the Fresh supermarket tour. The juice is now delivered before we even make it to the store, so Bennett and Beau can work together to make sure samples are prepared and ready. It also makes set-up and tear-down much quicker. I upload a couple more pictures for Gramps, click send, and then close my laptop.

Warren hasn't texted me since he left a few days ago. Honestly, I've been too busy to think much about it, but I am worried about him. It must have been a pretty bad family emergency for him to leave so quickly and not call.

Drew continues to follow me around with the camera. My little dot on the website continues to move all over the Midwest, from Indiana to Illinois. We have stops planned in Missouri for tomorrow, and then we'll finish in Chicago for the Black and White Ball.

The ball doubles as a fundraiser for the National Watermelon Association and will close the Fresh grocery store campaign. The who's who of the industry will be there, as well as a lot of donors, who want to support the agricultural community. I lean back to rest, letting the wheels of the bus eat the miles to our next location.

Chapter 19

THE HOTEL'S BALLROOM IS STUNNING. Crystal chandeliers drape from the ceiling, casting specks of light everywhere. The entire room is done in varying shades of black, white, gray, and silver. White tablecloths flutter over the tables. Jet black plates are lined with silver trim. Black napkins with silver swirly accents rest on top of the plates. The centerpieces are large vases with black and white feathers sticking out. The only concession to adding color are the red roses that cascade down the vases. Each vase has over a dozen roses. The aroma of fresh flowers fills the room, while small, white candles flicker around the base of the vases.

I smooth down the front of my dress and walk toward the drink station. The wait staff are all dressed in black pants and button-down shirts with gray vests and ties. Several walk around, carrying trays with all kinds of yummy treats.

"May I help you?" the attendant asks.

"A Shirley Temple, please."

He quickly begins making my drink. I take it and turn to survey the room. All of the queens are easy to spot. We're the only ones dressed in white. Everyone else is wearing black. The women have various lengths and styles, but they all wear black, while the men wear tuxes. Mr. and Mrs. Baron sit at the table with several influential people. From the looks on their faces, they are having a great time. Mrs. Baron laughs at something one of them say, and Mr. Baron puts his arm around her chair.

Most of the queens stand together in a group with some of the donors' and farmers' sons. Bennett and Beau are part of that group—along with V, Rosanne, Audrey, and Becca. Noelle is at a table with her father. He seems to be talking with a few wealthy patrons about something. Noelle looks bored, but, like me, she doesn't want to hang out with the group.

I actually got to talk to Gramps today. I spent the entire time trying to hide how bummed I am that Warren isn't going to be at the ball tonight. That was the one and only text I got from him over the last seven days, which is a little sketchy. But he's not the type to blow someone off—or, at least, I don't think he is. Our watermelon shipments keep arriving from them, so I know the farm is doing okay. Gramps could tell something was up, but he thought it had to do with the accident. I can honestly say it's not that anymore. Being with Warren and the Barons has helped me to start really living again. Sure, there are times that I miss my parents and Luke more than others, but Beau's fortune cookie intervention has taught me one thing—I have to keep going. I owe it to them to make something of myself by seeing what God has planned for my life.

The DJ has kept a steady stream of music playing, but no one has taken to the dance floor yet. That won't happen until the parade of the queens. It sounds a little more barbaric than it is. Basically, each queen and her sponsor take to the floor and waltz.

I make eye contact with Noelle, and she meets me by one of the seating areas.

"Your dress is amazing," I tell her.

It's one-shouldered with white, chiffon fabric gathered at the shoulder. A rhinestone broach holds the fabric together. The fabric flows down and gathers at the waist, where sequins and rhinestones make a belt that ties in the front with long, sparkly streamers down the front of her dress. She pulled her hair up on top of her head, under a rhinestone headband.

"Thanks."

"Seriously, you could just add wings, and you'd look like an angel," I remark.

"Well, you look gorgeous, too." She gestures towards my dress.

"Thanks, but it's all Mrs. Baron."

The dress has sheer, elbow-length sleeves that are white with rhinestones attached on the cuff in three rows. The sheer, white sleeve material circles around my neck and then goes down in a deep V in the back. The rest of the dress is done in white satin. The front has a heart-shaped neckline with rhinestones that outline along the edge, where the sheer fabric meets the satin. It fits my figure, then fluffs out so that I look like a mermaid at the bottom. A large rhinestone belt sits at my waist. Mrs. Baron insisted that I pull my hair up in a large bun that sits on top of my head. She added red lipstick and large chandelier earrings that I'm pretty sure will stretch my ear lobes down to my shoulders by the end of the night.

"We should probably join the other group of queens," I suggest.

"You're right. I just didn't want to face Bennett," she says.

"What do you mean?"

"I don't know. He won our last argument, and I don't want to be around him while he gloats."

"Do you like him? I mean, really like him?" I ask.

She looks out at the group he's in and pulls a face.

"We're too different."

"Let me tell you what Gramps always says. Oil and vinegar apart are hard to stomach; but shake 'em together, and you've got great salad dressing."

"Did you really just compare us to salad dressing?"

"Okay, so I know it sounds dumb, but the idea behind it isn't. Besides, I'm pretty sure he's into you. I've never seen a girl get under his skin like you do."

"We'll see, but, anyway, how's the watermelon juice business?"

"Great! We're selling it just as fast as we are making it. I'm hoping we'll be able to keep up with the demand once we have the real product launch party, and the commercial starts airing on TV."

"I'm sure you guys will do great. By the way, I'm dying to know what the commercial looks like. I can't wait."

"I really don't know. They took so many different shots that your guess is as good as mine."

The DJ turns the music down and calls for all of the queens to get ready for the parade. We all line up on one side of the dance floor and wait for our name to be called. As we are introduced, we each take a turn around the dance floor, then we all finish the waltz together. Mr. Baron still isn't a hundred percent with his leg, so he sent Bennett instead.

"Having fun?" he asks.

"I am. I had an interesting conversation with Noelle, though."

"What about?"

"Why do you want to know?"

Bennett sidesteps another couple and whirls us around to the other side of the dance floor.

"You've gotten better at waltzing," he remarks, ignoring my question.

"I've been practicing. Are you going to answer my question?"

"Which one?"

"Never mind. I guess I won't share with you what I know," I tease airily, hoping he will take the bait.

"I just want to know. Okay?"

"Fine, I'll tell you. I think she's into you, but she thinks you aren't into her. I used Gramp's oil and vinegar—"

"Please tell me you didn't use the salad dressing analogy that your grandfather uses for everything." His eyes beg me to tell him no.

"I may have done that."

"Did she look at you like you're insane? No one uses that saying, unless they're eighty."

"You're just embarrassed, and I haven't even gotten to the good part yet."

He looks at me expectantly as we continue to waltz across the floor for the final strains of the waltz.

"Thanks for the dance, bro," I turn and slowly walk off the dance floor, leaving Bennett to wonder about Noelle.

The dance floor is taken over by other couples, but all of the queens meet back by the auction tables. Each one of us is given a very expensive piece of jewelry to wear that will be auctioned off later tonight. I clasp an emerald and diamond necklace around my neck. It has three large emerald stones, with diamonds that circle around them, hanging down in a straight line, giving the necklace the letter Y shape. If it wasn't worth more than my entire college savings account, I'd be tempted to bid on it. Noelle has ruby bangles—some with ruby stones and others with diamonds. One has a large ruby heart that is suspended from it. Audrey is next with sapphire earrings that hang from small silver ropes. They are simple elegance. At least, those were the words the jeweler used when she put them on Audrey. The national queen, Becca, gets a diamond choker and a security guard to go with it because her piece is so expensive.

The rest of the girls finish getting their pieces and start walking the room. The jewelry is one of the main parts of tonight's auction. There are other things, too, like paintings and trips to Hawaii, but the jewelry will be the big moneymaker tonight.

Once we've all gotten our jewelry, we mingle among the guests to show off the pieces we're wearing. Several women want to look at Becca's. The idea that a security guard has to follow her around has caught the attention of several guests.

After circulating the room for a little while and making polite conversation with all the important people, I start to scan the room for V. I don't recognize the people she's with from any of our conventions, so that can only mean they're wealthy benefactors. I really just want to see how's she's doing, since her brother got stationed in Germany. But I decide to wait; it's not like we could really talk about it when she's with that crew, anyway.

The dance floor is crowded with couples, which makes me miss Warren. I order another Shirley Temple and have a seat on one of the sofas, twirling the cherry with the little straw stirrer they put in the drink.

"This seat taken?" a boy about my age asks. Everything about him screams expensive.

"No, help yourself." I motion to the opposite side of the sofa, but he sits right beside me.

"So, I was wondering if you'd like to dance with me?"

Trying to let him down easily, I offer, "Maybe later."

He nods in understanding.

"You are very beautiful," he says as he puts his arms around my shoulders on the back of the sofa.

I push him back a little. "I'm sorry if I gave you the wrong impression. And while I'm sure you're a *nice* guy, I have a boyfriend."

I get up and scan the room for Bennett or Beau. Bennett is actually talking to Noelle. Beau is walking right in front of the dance floor. I swerve toward the dance floor and snag Beau's arm.

"Dance with me," I demand, trying to drag him onto the dance floor.

He doesn't budge, which causes me to have to turn around.

"Come on."

"What is up with you?" he asks.

I don't have time to explain; the boy from the sofa is headed our way. Beau sees him and waves him over.

"Hey, Jack, long time. How's everything going?"

"You two know each other?" Of course, they would. I'm not that lucky.

"Went to camp together when we were kids," Jack says.

They do some secret camp handshake and laugh a little when they're done.

"Well, Jack, it was nice to meet you, but Beau owes me a dance."

I know I'm being a little rude, but he seemed a little too comfortable on the sofa, and I really just don't want to be in the same three-foot space.

"So, this is the boyfriend?"

"I'm not—"

I step on Beau's foot with my heel.

"Yup, she's my girlfriend," he manages with a look that is barely believable.

"Sorry to run off, but Beau owes me a dance." I drag Beau to the dance floor.

Beau spins me around before we start the dance. "Okay, what was that all about? You made me look like an idiot in front of a friend."

"I know. I am sorry about that part, but he was getting too friendly on the sofa. I had to act fast, and Bennett was talking with Noelle."

We dance until the end of the song and through the next one. An announcement is made for the start of the evening's meal, so we head off to find Mr. Baron's table. They start us off with brie, which is basically a block of cheese with apple slices, and a small cranberry and apple salad. The main course arrives next with a steak the size of our entire plate, garlic mashed potatoes, and glazed carrots. Dessert is watermelon sorbet.

Mrs. Baron and I excuse ourselves to go get ready for the auction. The queens will be traveling around the room, showing off the auction items. Mrs. Baron, Mr. Stone, and the national president, Mrs. Greene, all worked to put together the auction items, so they start passing them out to us in the order we'll go.

V starts first with a crystal vase with intricate floral patterns that run down the sides. Lightning-quick, the auctioneer already has the vase at upwards of two thousand dollars. It doesn't take long until the auctioneer yells, "Sold." V takes the item to the buyer and has them sign the paper invoice. Becca is next with a painting of a tractor and watermelon field. She works the room, waiting for it to be purchased. The auction is an hour in when they finally start with the queen's jewelry pieces. V's triple strands of pearls with the large flower broach goes for a crazy amount of money. She takes it to the buyer, everyone parting to make way for her because we all want to see who bought it.

Mr. Stone buys Noelle's bangles and then gives them to her publicly on the stage. It's a sweet father-daughter moment. For the first time in a long time, I'm able to watch it and feel only happiness. There was a time that watching those father-daughter moments reminded me that those moments for me are gone.

My necklace goes to an oil tycoon, whose daughter married a watermelon farmer. He signs the receipt, and I take it back to Mrs. Baron, who is too busy to even look up. She just smiles her thanks and continues with the auction items.

Rosanne's ring and bracelet are the last pieces to be auctioned off tonight. She stands in the center of the dance floor for a minute or two before she starts working her way around the room. The bids just keep going up. The ring is a yellow diamond with white diamonds surrounding it. The bracelet is similar with alternating yellow and white diamonds. Finally, the auctioneer closes out the item.

Everyone goes back to dancing and mingling. I just want to sit for a little while. I've been on my feet in heels for the last few hours, and they need a break. Beau sits down beside me.

"Doing okay?"

"My feet hurt, but other than that, I'm good."

"So, I'm calling in a return for that 'boyfriend favor' from earlier."

"You are?"

"Yup, it's easy. Go dance with Bennett."

I look around the room to find him. He's getting a drink from the drink station.

"Why?"

"Just trust me."

I roll my eyes, but I get up to go ask Bennett to dance with me. We hit the dance floor with other couples, who are dancing to a slow song.

"No Warren, huh?" Bennett asks.

"Nope. He texted to say he couldn't come."

"I'm sorry. But, hey, you've got me, and I'm pretty cool."

"Pretty cool." I make my voice sound bored and my eyes big and round.

"Hi, guys," Beau says. He's dancing with Noelle.

"Hey," I say, catching onto Beau's plan.

"Grace, I need to ask you a question about something you said from earlier. Bennett, swap partners with me."

Bennett looks at me, and I wink, so he knows we've both been in on this little trick. I raise my arm and twirl into Beau's arms. Beau does the same thing with Noelle, landing her safely into Bennett's arms.

"That was so much fun," I whisper to Beau.

"Shhh, let's listen to them."

"I think they've thrown us together on purpose," Bennett says.

"I think you're right," Noelle says.

"Listen—" they both say at the same time, then stop. Bennett looks over at me and Beau.

"Okay, you two have done your part. Now go dance somewhere else."

He's smiling, and so is Noelle; so when Beau whirls us to the opposite side of the floor, I don't complain.

"I'm surprised at you. Good idea, though."

"I just hope it works. Bennett has been moping around these last few weeks. I'm hoping they can work it out."

"Beau?"

"Yeah?"

"Seriously, I can't feel my feet anymore. Can we sit down somewhere?"

We head to the table where we sat for our meal and grab a seat. I resist the urge to take my shoes off and rub my feet. We have only a few more minutes before the ball is over, but people have already started to find their coats and head for the door.

When the final guest leaves, Mrs. Baron, Mr. Stone, and Mrs. Greene sit at a table, pouring over the numbers from the auction. Bennett and Noelle sit with us, while Mr. Baron kisses Mrs. Baron good night and heads to bed. We have to wait another twenty minutes before Mrs. Baron is finished totaling numbers. But it's worth it because the ball was a huge success.

I head to my room, tired but excited. We get to go home tomorrow. I'll get to sleep in my own bed again; and, after all of those days on the tour bus, I can't wait to stay in just one place for a couple of days.

Chapter 20

MRS. BARON HAS BEEN GOING a hundred miles an hour, trying to keep up with the Watermelon Nectar launch party and trying to get everything ready for the Watermelon Festival. So, the boys and I offered to take over the Watermelon Festival duties.

Mr. Baron invited Mr. Stone and Noelle to join us for a couple of days, too. They will be staying in the extra rooms above the office in the old farmhouse. Beau is at the airport picking them up now, as their flight should have landed about an hour ago.

Bennett has been overseeing the splat zone for the manmade, gigantic, eighteen-foot, five-hundred-pound watermelon that is suspended from a crane. A lever will be pulled tonight to officially start the festival. Forty watermelons will drop to the ground from a trap door in the watermelon. Once the melons hit the splat zone, the fireworks will start.

Vendors will line the streets tonight, selling everything from food to watermelon trinkets and glow sticks. Their white tents sit waiting for tonight's festivities to begin. I've been working on the stage for the festival queen contest and the largest watermelon contest that will take place tomorrow. Large ferns line the front of the stage. I've stuck large, glittery, cardboard watermelons in the ferns.

They should shimmer in the lights tonight. A white background with red, draped fabric is the backdrop.

There's a 5K watermelon run tomorrow morning, too. I check my clipboard to see what all I still have left to do. So far, only two items have been checked off my list. I feel like the bees we put in the fields to pollinate the plants. I move from one thing to another, never stopping.

The town hall volunteers and I have coordinated decorations. They are busy hanging green lights in the trees. Large watermelon banners have been hung from the street lamps that run down Main Street.

Beau pulls up with the Stones while I'm organizing the games for tomorrow's relay races. Noelle hops out of the car and hurries over to the game station.

"Hi. Perfect timing," I tell her.

"What can I help you with?"

"Organizing the equipment for the races. Can you count to make sure we have an equal number of everything here?"

"Will do," she says, as she starts separating the sacks for the three-legged race.

Beau and Mr. Stone join us while we're still at the games station.

"Did you enjoy your tour?" I ask Mr. Stone.

"I did. I can't wait to see the watermelon drop. I know they've talked about it on the news."

"They did a piece on the local news last year," I say.

"I think they're sending someone from a national affiliate to broadcast the drop tonight," Beau says, putting his hands in his pockets.

I turn to Mr. Stone. "Have you had a chance to check out the eighteen-foot watermelon?"

"Beau was just getting ready to show me," Mr. Stone says.

"Awesome. Let me know if you have any questions. The largest watermelon competition starts later today," I remind him.

"I'll be there, ready to judge," he promises.

Then, he and Beau head toward the watermelon and the roped-off splat zone.

I leave Noelle to finish the game station and head toward the face painting area. The tables are already covered with red and white checkered tablecloths. Stencils and paint take up both ends of the table so that two kids can get their faces painted at the same time.

Finally, everything is checked off my list, and I'm able to head back to get ready for the opening ceremony and watermelon drop. I've texted Warren off and on throughout the last few days. The closest confirmation I've gotten that he's coming is his brief text that said *I'm on it.* Not sure if he meant on a plane or that he's trying to get here. Either way, that was the last I've heard from him. I don't know if I should be angry or worried. He's been very vague lately.

I put on my pink, scalloped-edged shorts that have little watermelons at the ends of the scallops and a mint green, flowy tank top. It's going to be hot outside, so I put my hair in a high bun and let a few pieces hang free. I choose white, sparkly flip flops to complete the look. I grab my crown and sash on my way out and drive to the Barons' house.

We all arrive at the festival together. The vendors are going in full force. People are buying all kinds of food and watermelon treats. In a few minutes, I'll start the watermelon-eating contest, which Mr. Baron and Mr. Stone both have agreed to compete in.

The stage is set with a large rectangular table and plastic table-cloth. Watermelon halves lay open in front of ten chairs. Each man is given a plastic trash bag with the center cut out to put their head through. That way, they should stay mostly clean.

The city council president makes a few opening remarks, and then he invites Mrs. Baron and me to the stage to kick off the festivities.

Mrs. Baron takes the mic.

"Gentlemen, please take your seat." She instructs all of the contestants on where to sit.

Mr. Baron and Mr. Stone—along with the other eight competitors, who are all in their plastic trash bags—swish and crackle their way up to their seats.

"Gentlemen, whoever finishes his half of the watermelon first wins, but remember, you can't use your hands," Mrs. Baron continues to speak into the mic. "On your mark, get set, go!"

The men dig face-first into their halves. The watermelons move and slide around, so they have to use their heads to slide it back in front of them. The crowd cheers on their favorites loudly. Mr. Baron has a watermelon seed stuck in the middle of his forehead, but he keeps on eating. I walk up and down the row, checking to see how each one is doing.

In the middle of the table, a man stands up and throws his arms in the air. I hurry down to see that he's finished the melon. He's eaten it clear to the rind. He has watermelon juice dribbling down his chin.

Chunks of watermelon stick to his face and in his beard, but the crowd loves it. I turn the watermelon, so the crowd can see it's empty. More cheers erupt. Mrs. Baron brings him a roll of paper towels to clean up after she puts several rolls on the table for the other men who are also in various degrees of mess.

I present our winner with a trophy that has a watermelon on the top of it.

"Our watermelon-eating champion," I announce into the mic.

He raises the trophy again to more cheers.

A few council member volunteers begin clearing off the stage, so that we can have the festival queen contest. While they are cleaning, I call the judges forward for the largest watermelon contest. The competitors placed their entries in front of the stage earlier today, so now all they have to do is line up to watch the judges. Mr. Stone and the city council president first measure the length and diameter of each watermelon. Then, very carefully, they have the owner of each watermelon roll it onto the scale to see how much the melon weighs. Mr. Stone records the information on a clipboard I gave him earlier. He and the council president talk for a few minutes, looking over the clipboard. They give first place to the melon that weighed ninety-five pounds. Second and third place ribbons are passed out, too, and then the judges line up with the winners to get a picture made.

The competition took just long enough to get the stage set up for the pageant. Noelle and two other ladies from the watermelon community sit at the judges' table. They are supposed to judge the girls on stage presence and their speaking ability when they answer their onstage question.

The girls are all dressed in various watermelon-ish outfits in varying shades of red, green, pink, and white. Mrs. Baron calls each one of them up individually and says a few things about them while they walk the stage, modeling their outfit. When a contestant makes it to the center of the stage, I meet them and ask them a question. I try to smile reassuringly at them. I remember what it was like not too long ago. Even though this is an entirely different pageant than mine, the girls' nerves are sure to be in full force. Having to talk on stage can be nerve-racking, especially if you've never done it before. Luckily, tonight they all are able to answer the question I ask.

We call all the girls back on stage when the last contestant finishes her question. Noelle brings Mrs. Baron the envelope with our winner's name in it. Mrs. Baron opens the envelope. Then, she steps up to the mic.

"Ladies and gentlemen, your new watermelon festival queen is . . . Millie Brown."

Millie steps forward as the crowd cheers for her. Last year's queen puts a tiara on her head and a sash around her shoulders. Millie smiles and waves in excitement. She's cute in her light green dress that hits right above her knees, and black high heels that have rhinestone watermelons on them. The heels match the black belt at her waist. Millie's first duty will be to start the 5K run, which is next on today's agenda. The run will finish just in time to do the watermelon drop and fireworks.

Noelle, Mrs. Baron, and I head over with Millie to the starting line of the race. Runners are stretching and jogging in place to get loose and wake up their muscles before the start of the run. Mrs. Baron hands Millie the air horn and the microphone.

Millie puts the mic to her mouth and says, "Runners, on your mark." Everyone takes their starting position.

"Get set . . . GO!" Millie yells while pressing the air horn.

The runners take off in a mass. We watch them for a little while before heading to the vendors. We have a few minutes before we have to head up the games, and I want to see how the Watermelon Nectar booth is doing. Beau volunteered to work the booth for us. Some of the field hands and Raul wanted a few extra hours, so they're helping out, too. Raul's wife is expecting their fourth child, and he needs the extra money. I know the Barons have been putting a little extra aside for them and plan to give it to Raul when the baby is born.

There's a steady stream of customers at the booth. It looks like the juice has been selling pretty steadily.

"How's it going?" I ask Beau.

He hands a customer three bottles of the juice.

"Pretty good. People seem to like it."

"How much more do we have in the truck?" Mrs. Baron asks.

"The truck's still about half-full. We ought to last through the event."

"We should hand it out to the runners at the end of the race," I suggest.

"Good idea. The news crews should be there, too. It could be some free publicity," Mrs. Baron says.

"Can we spare a case?" I look to Beau for the answer. He's been working the booth the last few hours. He'd have the best handle on how much we have left.

"I think it's worth possibly not having enough at the end of the night," Beau says, shrugging.

He takes the towel he had on his shoulder and throws it to Raul. He was using it to wipe off the bottles before he handed them to a customer.

"You're in charge, Raul. I'm going to carry a case over to the finish line. Besides, it's a Baron tradition to do the three-legged race. We'll grab Bennett on our way over."

We leave Mrs. Baron and the juice at the finish line and head over to the game station to find Noelle expertly handling the games.

"Who won the race last year?" Noelle asked.

"We both did. We raced together," Beau says, pointing between Bennett, who is some ways off working the splat zone, and himself.

"I think you're going to be disappointed this year. The rules have changed," Noelle says.

"How so?" Beau asks.

"Noelle made the rule that the teams who won last year can't race together this year." I smirk, waiting to hear his reply.

"Who put her in charge?"

"I did. I was doing too many things. I needed her help."

Bennett is talking to some of the police officers who are guarding the perimeter of the splat zone with him. Beau hollers at him.

"Bennett, three-legged race."

That's all it takes, and Bennett heads over to join us.

"Hi," he says, looking directly at Noelle.

She smiles up at him.

"Hi."

"You're not going to believe this. Your girlfriend here," Beau points at Noelle, and then goes on, "changed the rules for the race. We can't race together." He crosses his arms, pretending to be angry.

Neither one of them put up a fight when Beau calls Noelle Bennett's girlfriend. Bennett just asks, "Did she now?"

I make a mental note to have a girl-to-girl chat with Noelle later tonight. Today just got a little more exciting. At least, I can focus on their love story, since Warren hasn't shown up today.

"So, who are you boys going to race with?" I ask.

"I'm pretty sure I can find someone willing to help me out," Bennett says, smiling at Noelle.

"Oh, you can, can you?" she asks.

Bennett puts his arm around her shoulders, and they walk toward the game station.

"When did that happen?"

"The night of the ball," Beau says.

"When we made them dance together?"

"I like to say we helped them along. 'Made' sounds like we forced them, when you and I both know it was coming."

"We make a good team." I put my hand up for a high-five.

"We do." He high-fives me back, slapping his palm into mine. "Want to give those two a run for their money in the race?"

"Let's do it."

Noelle leads several other games first to keep the kids busy. She has a balloon toss and bob-for-plastic-watermelon-pieces game that is a hit with the younger crowd. She does a ring toss for the kids, too. Finally, it's time for the sack races.

Noelle does a shorter version for the younger kids. Some hop down, while others do the traditional method of one leg, then the middle leg, in the sack. Several fall and get back up laughing, but the winners are two little boys who clearly are brothers with their matching red hair and freckles. They jump up and down in excitement when Noelle gives them their ribbon.

At some point, Mr. Baron and Mrs. Baron make their way over to watch the boys. A council volunteer and Millie take Noelle's place of judging the adult sack race. Noelle and Bennett shove their leg down the sack and wrap their arms around each other's waists. Beau and I do the same and hold tight to the center of the sack. We get in line with six other couples.

The air horn blasts, and we take off. Bennett and Noelle are ahead of us. But Bennett needs to slow down, or Noelle's not going to be able to keep up; her legs are much shorter than his. Beau matches his stride with mine, making me thankful for his thoughtfulness and that I'm not being dragged across the field. We half-run, half-gallop toward the finish line.

Bennett takes too big a step, causing Noelle to lose her balance, so they go down long enough for us to pass them. There are still several couples ahead of us, and the odds of winning at this point for either one of us isn't good. Beau and I finish in fourth place. We yell for Bennett and Noelle. Bennett has basically picked Noelle up by the side, and he is partly-dragging, partly-carrying her to the finish line. They're laughing more than they're trying to win at this point. They cross the finish line with one couple behind them.

"Great way to catch up," I say to Bennett.

He looks down at Noelle and shrugs.

"I should have thought about our height difference more before I took off like a crazy man." He gives her a quick squeeze.

"It's okay; we made up time after we fell," she says and giggles. I can barely believe my ears. There's definitely been a change.

The adult three-legged race closes out the games for the game station, and most of the 5K runners have completed the race. There were several walkers in the race, too, so we still have a good half hour before we need to be back for the watermelon drop. Mrs. Baron shoos us off to go look at the vendors. She's got Mr. Baron and Millie overseeing the seed-spitting contest, and she's passing out the Watermelon Nectar as the runners cool down around the finish line. Hopefully, the camera catches one of the runners drinking the juice.

Bennett grabs Noelle's hand and heads off toward the vendors, making me miss Warren. I push the unwanted feelings away and focus on the fun. Beau and I follow behind them a step or two.

"So, no Warren?"

"No."

"Don't you think it's a bit weird? He shows up, gets you to sign the contract, then suddenly has to go back home."

"We've texted back and forth," I snap. It comes out sounding way more defensive than I would have liked.

He says nothing at first, letting the silence grate on my nerves. But eventually, his annoyance wins out.

"When are you going to wake up and see it?" he asks, frustration oozing out of him.

"I do see it. So much more than you realize," I huff out. "I see that you don't like him and that you're doing everything you can to make things difficult for me."

"He's using you, Grace. Get it through your head. Why else would he give you so much attention?"

I suck in my breath. His words sting worse than those raindrops that pelted us on our run from the truck.

Almost instantly, Beau realizes what he said.

"Grace, I—"

He reaches out to me, but I swipe his arm away.

"I think you made your point."

I turn to walk away.

"Please, wait." He follows after me. "Of course, anyone would want to spend time with you. You're funny and smart and—"

"You think I'm smart?"

"Yes . . . focus on what I'm saying here. Warren is not telling you the truth. I don't want to see you hurt. No one does. Be careful. Okay?"

A small part of me has worried the same thing lately. Warren has been a bit shady, but now that Beau is saying it out loud, I don't want to think about it at all. I ignore that uneasy feeling slicing though my stomach and say, "He said it was a family thing. I don't want to be nosy."

"I'll leave you alone about it. Just think about what I'm saying is all," Beau says.

I can tell he's still irritated about it, but he lets it go.

We all stop at the balloon dart games and play a couple of rounds. Noelle comes away with a stuffed bear dressed up to look like a watermelon slice. We wander from vendor to vendor, letting Noelle lead the way. This is her first southern Indiana watermelon festival. For the boys and me, the sights and sounds are old news. She spots the watermelon popsicle stand, so we head there next. I order my favorite watermelon slushy, while the boys and Noelle get popsicles shaped and flavored like watermelon.

"We'd better head back; it's getting close to the drop," I say, looking at my phone's clock.

Everyone agrees, and we eat our treats on the way. People have started to gather around the roped-off area. Blankets and lawn chairs are set up all over the lawn at the end of Main Street. The security guards now walk the perimeter to keep people out of harm's way.

Mr. and Mrs. Baron are already on the platform with the city officials. Millie waits at the bottom of the stairs for me.

"Are you ready?" I ask her.

"Yes, I'm excited." She bounces up and down on her heels.

The boys and Noelle head to find Mr. Stone. He's been guarding a good spot for them on the lawn.

Millie and I walk up to the podium, and I grab the mic.

"Ladies and Gentlemen, let's start the countdown, ten . . . nine . . . eight . . . seven," I motion for the crowd to stay with me, "six . . . five . . ."

I trail off at the mic, but the crowd continues to count. Millie and I hold tight to the rope, and when the crowd says zero, we pull with all of our might. The trap door at the bottom of the melon opens, and forty watermelons plummet to the ground with loud thunks and splats. Some of the closer spectators are even hit with flying juice and seeds.

Fireworks erupt in the background. The crowd oohs and aahs from the show of the fireworks. As the night winds down, I wonder about the Watermelon Nectar booth. I'll have to check the numbers with Raul and Mrs. Baron tomorrow, but I'm pretty sure the booth had a successful night, which can mean only great things for our first launch party in Chicago. Mrs. Baron has been frantically pulling all the loose ends together to be ready for the launch next week.

I find Noelle and the boys in the crowd and wave them toward me. I'm ready to go home. Another watermelon festival can be marked off as a success.

Chapter 21

THE DAY OF THE LAUNCH is here, and all I can think about is that I'm going to get to see Warren today. He promised he'd be here. Part of me wants to tell Beau, "I told you so," but my inner-adult keeps me in check.

The convention center has been set up with a stage and a runway. Round tables are scattered throughout the space with light lime green tablecloths. The chairs have the same colored ribbon tied around them in big bows. The centerpieces are basically floral arrangements that have a Watermelon Nectar bottle sticking out of the top of them. Large posters hang from every available space in the room. For the official launch poster, they chose the one of Beau and me holding hands, drinking the juice. They've managed to make one large enough to span across the back of the stage, creating a backdrop. Waiters will be walking around serving the juice from silver trays, too.

The media section has been roped off, and informational flyers have been placed in each one of their seats. One of the things that took so much of Mrs. Baron's time was creating the press release kit, which has the flyer, product information, links to the digital poster, and contact information, as well as where the juice can be purchased. She spent hours on that part alone.

She insisted on a coral carpet for the guests to arrive on and created logo backdrops for photo ops. The attire for tonight is formal—so formal that Beau and I had custom outfits created to complement one another. Thanks to the poster and commercial, Beau and I now get to share the spotlight for tonight's release and possibly more release parties in other cities if this one goes well.

I pick at a piece of lint on the front of my dress. Beau and I seem to be thrown together so much lately. It's not really all that bad, but he seems to always be there when I need him, too. It's all just complicated.

Beau has on a black tuxedo with gray pinstripes and a coral pocket square. My dress is gray with coral accents along the heart-shaped neckline. I have huge coral dangly earrings and a coral ring that is on loan from Mrs. Baron.

The hair and makeup artist gave me a very glamorous look tonight. My hair has been curled and left to flow down my back with the side pieces twisted and pulled in softly. My eye shadow was done in contrasting shades of gray and silver with black winged eyeliner to top it off.

Beau and I have been given rooms behind the convention center in a corridor. We are supposed to wait until someone comes and gets us before we walk the runway. I can either stare at myself in the mirror or pace back and forth while I wait. A knock sounds on my door. I look at the clock on my phone. It's too early for us to head up to the party, so I peek around the corner of my door.

A security guard stands there, looking amused and holding some roses.

"A special delivery," he says, handing me the flowers.

They smell amazing. I take them and place them on the dressing table in the room, pulling the card as I do. They're from Warren. There's a card wishing me good luck tonight sticking out of the top of them. I don't know why everyone is so against him. Sure, he was a little distant these last few weeks, but it's not like he'd send me roses if he wasn't into me.

My phone rings, and the caller ID shows that it's Gramps. I answer it right away.

"Hello," I answer.

Static buzzes through the phone as Gramps says, "Hi, Short Stack."

"Just a minute. I can't hear you," I say, opening the door to my room and heading down the walkway, trying to find a better signal.

We play the *Can you hear me now?* game, trying to find a good connection. I turn corner after corner, zigzagging every which way, until I finally find a spot where the signal is clear.

"I hear you have a big night," Gramps says.

"Yeah, I'm excited. My dress is amazing. The posters are so cool. I can't wait to see the commercial."

We talk more about what's happing here. Then, Gramps tells me about the villagers and the progress he's making.

"Only two more weeks, and I'll be home, Short Stack." He sounds tired, but I can tell it's a good tired.

"I know. I miss you."

"I miss you, too."

We talk for a little bit longer before saying our goodbyes. I disconnect and look around, trying to remember which way I went when trying to find a signal. I round the corner to a spot that's unfamiliar. A boy and girl are walking hand-in-hand several steps ahead of me.

"Excuse me," I holler, but they just keep going.

I step up my pace and try to catch them. Hopefully, they'll know where we are and can point me in the right direction, back to my room. The guy turns his head a little bit. I must be missing Warren more than I realize because he looks just like him.

"Warren?" I holler.

But they're still too far away. They turn the corner, so I pick up the front of my dress and run as best I can in my high heels.

What I see when I round the corner stops me dead in my tracks. It's Warren all right, and he's got his lips pressed to someone else's. I can't hold in the gasp that escapes my mouth. They both snap their heads away from one another and look at me. Recognition snaps into place on Warren's face. He steps away from the girl, looking a little surprised to see me.

"Grace, how did you . . . I mean, I thought you were backstage."

He backpedals, ending up making it sound almost like a question.

"I got your roses." I resolve not to give him even an inkling as to how I really feel and fight to keep my voice even.

He steps back toward the girl he's been kissing.

Then, like we've entered an alternate universe, he says, "Good. Grace, this is Sarah. Sarah, Grace."

He points to each of us during his introduction, his composure back in place.

"I've heard so much about you," she says, making my stomach roll with dread.

My mask of indifference slips a notch. I look at Warren. He doesn't seem the least bit sorry for cheating, only for being caught.

"But I thought, we were—"

I drop off what I was saying. I don't really know what we were, other than that he made me feel special and wanted. I thought I'd done the same for him.

"I thought you understood. We were just having fun."

He looks at me, surprised that I didn't understand about our relationship—if it can even be called that. Sarah wraps her arms around Warren's waist. He does nothing to stop her, so I wrap my arms around my middle, hunching over a little. Everyone was right. It's just a game to him. I was a game. Chills run down my entire body. Visiting when they were in the running for the contract was planned. Beau was right. Warren was using me. I gather what dignity I have left and stand up straight.

"Tell me this: did you come on the tour with me to seal the deal with the contract?"

"Obviously. But hey, we had a fun run." He acts like he's surprised I even had to ask.

I am so stupid. I totally fell for that smile of his and what I thought was southern charm. I can't believe I was so dumb. With the last bit of strength I have left inside, I say, "Thank you for the roses. Please don't try to contact me again. Any business can be done through your father and Mr. Baron. Goodbye, Warren Hartley."

Head held high, I walk away. I refuse to give him any reaction. I keep it together until I turn the corner. The realization that Warren willingly backed over my heart for a melon load of watermelon hits in full force, and the sobs start racking my body. I blindly wander the corridors until I find my room.

The first thing I see is the vase of roses from Warren. I grab it and throw it in the trashcan as hard as I can. The vase shatters, and pieces fly out. Just great. *Shattered vase meets shattered heart,* I think to myself as I bend down and try to pick up most of the jagged pieces. A small sliver cuts my finger, which starts a whole new round of tears. I put my finger in my mouth, trying to stop the blood flow from getting on my dress, and cry even harder. I find a towel they used to cover me with earlier today during my hair and makeup session and wrap it around my finger. Defeated, I sit in my chair and just let the sobs take over.

A knock on the door reminds me of what I still have to do tonight. I grab another tissue, trying to fix the mess that is my face. The knocking is more intense now, so I get up and head to the door. I check my makeup in the mirror on my way. I shouldn't have looked. I look worse than I thought. My nose is red from crying, and my eyeliner looks like a black ink pen exploded on my face. Beau peeks in before I can make it to the door.

"Grace! What happened?" he asks, coming into the room.

I stand there, not bothering to stop the black waterfalls of my mascara from running down my cheeks.

Beau puts his hands on my shoulders and gives me a little shake to snap me out of my silent trance.

"You were right. Okay?"

The tears start to fall freely from my eyes again, mixing with my mascara and crisscrossing down my cheeks. I dab at them with my mangled tissue and sit back down in my chair.

"What do you mean?"

He sits beside me in the other chair, doing that awkward comforting, pat thing that guys do when girls are crying, and they don't know what to do.

"Warren."

It's the only word I can get out.

He starts texting on his phone.

"What are you doing?" I ask.

"Calling the makeup crew back in here. We've got twenty minutes to put you back together."

"You go. I can't."

"No."

He stands up.

"No?"

"Warren isn't going to rob you of this moment. We'll do it together. I'm not going out there without you."

He reaches down and takes my hand. Then, he pulls me up, wrapping me in a bear hug, which is the last thing I want right now. I cry harder. I want to hit something or scream or maybe both. Because there are so many emotions churning around inside me right now, I feel like I could explode.

He refuses to let go until he feels my shoulders relax, and the sobs stop. I stand there, my face in his chest, just breathing in and out.

"Why didn't I listen to you?" I moan, angry at myself for being so oblivious.

"That's a question for another day. Right now, you just need to focus on you and the fact that about two thousand people and the media are waiting to see the Watermelon Nectar commercial and you."

He still has his hands on my shoulders when someone clears her throat in the doorway. Beau and I look over at the same time to see the makeup artist.

He lets his arms drop.

She takes one look at me and says, "What did you do?"

"Long story. Can you fix it?" I ask, only slightly sniffling now.

"Yes. We'll have you ready."

She looks at Beau.

"You go away, so we can get to business."

Beau turns to look at me.

"Will you be okay?" he asks.

"Yes, but will you come and get me when it's time?" I hate how weak my voice sounds.

"I will," he promises before the make-up artist shoos Beau out of the room and gets right to work. She puts eye drops in my eyes to get rid of the redness and touches up everything. She's in fast-forward mode, barely laying down one brush before picking up the other. She adds one last layer of lip gloss when Beau walks through the door.

"Wow, you look much better."

We both turn and give him the *did you really just say that* look.

"I mean, you're a miracle worker," he says to the makeup artist.

My jaw drops open even further. Beau is usually pretty good at words when he wants to be. What's gotten into him tonight?

"I mean, you're beautiful."

I take pity on him.

"It's okay. I know I ugly cried. You're just trying to be nice."

"I mean, I wouldn't call it ugly cried—"

"Beau, stop while you're ahead," I warn.

He smiles and offers me his hand. I take it. His hand is warm and comforting. There's something else, too, but I can't place what it is. We walk through the back corridors to the back of the stage. Mrs. Baron is giving the opening remarks. Beau and I wait for our cue.

"Grace?' Beau whispers.

"Yeah?"

"You look stunning tonight."

"I believe that's because the makeup artist is a miracle worker—your words, not mine."

I pick on him a little.

"Not my smoothest moment."

I laugh a little, which is surprising, considering I just saw my boyfriend kissing another girl.

"True, but I appreciate the effort."

I squeeze his hand just as the music swells in volume to mark our entrance. Beau and I walk through the curtains to thunderous applause. We walk the runway hand-in-hand and stop at the end of the runway, where two bottles of Watermelon Nectar are waiting on us. We grab them and do the same pose that is on the flyers and advertisements. Flashbulbs go off in a blinding number. When the flashes die down, Beau and I turn and walk back to the podium. We face the teleprompter. Beau's line is first.

"Ladies and Gentlemen, we are so excited to be here tonight." He reads from the screen.

"Beau and I have been working really hard on this commercial. We would love to share it with you if you'd like."

The crowd erupts. I see Warren in the corner; he raises his bottle in a salute. Beau must have seen him, too, because he puts his arm around me for reassurance. I lean into him, glad for the support.

Beau reads from the teleprompter again.

"And now, we give you the first preview of Watermelon Nectar's introductory commercial!"

A large screen comes down from the center of the ceiling, and the lights go out. Beau and I take our seats in the audience next to Bennett and Noelle. She flew in to be a part of tonight. Music starts playing, and I'm running through the watermelon field with my dress billowing behind me. I look over my shoulder. The camera spans to Beau, and then it's us running hand-in-hand. He picks me up, twirling me around, and then carries me to what was a green screen, but now, in the commercial, has been digitally enhanced to look like the setting sun. He plays his part well—almost too well. The look on his face looks like a boy in love. Like, really in love. I almost wonder if he's really acting. The camera switches angles again, and Beau sets me down. The last frame of the film is Beau and me looking at one another, while someone says, "Watermelon Nectar—because life should be beautiful and sweet."

The lights go back up, and the audience is silent for a moment, like they've been affected by the romance in the commercial. Then, Beau and I are met with applause as we head back to the stage. The teleprompter has to restart Beau's line twice before the audience's applause is quiet enough to be heard.

"We want to thank you for coming tonight. We know the media will have questions for us, and we will gladly take a few of those now."

Mrs. Baron joins us on the stage. Most of the questions are directed at her. She answers which cities we plan to have more release parties in and what stores Watermelon Nectar can be found in. I zone out and just let her do the talking. After the emotional rollercoaster of this evening, I'm wiped out.

Beau nudges me, snapping me out of my mentally numb trance. I look up, and the crowd is staring at me. I look at Beau with wide eyes.

"So, are you going to keep us waiting? Everyone wants to know what you thought of working with me during the commercial," Beau says, saving me.

He did it in a way that didn't let on that I wasn't paying attention, too. The list just gets longer of all the things I'm going to owe him for after tonight.

"Beau and I go way back. Most of the time was fun. If anything, it was more dangerous for Beau. Why don't you tell them about the time I almost took you out during the shoot?" I prompt him.

He takes over and tells the story to the crowd. The media eats it up, and he has everyone laughing. It's a great way to close the question and answer portion of the night out.

Beau and I pose one last time with a juice bottle in our hand. Then, we turn and walk back up the runway and into the corridor. I lean against the wall, taking my shoes off. Mrs. Baron is giving them directions on how to head out and thanking them for coming.

"Grace?" Beau whispers my name as he walks towards me.

He's got the same look in his eyes as the night I ran away from him when we were in the truck.

"Yes." My breath gets caught in my throat.

I'm still leaning against the wall, so Beau leans in against the wall on one shoulder facing me.

"I'm proud of you." Beau looks down at me, a smile turning up the corners of his mouth.

"Thanks. You helped me a lot today. The crowd loved your story."

He chuckles a little. But his face gets serious again.

"There's something I've got to say."

He reaches over and brushes a stand of my hair off my face. My heart starts to beat faster than I ever thought possible.

"There is?"

It comes out breathier than I wanted it to.

"It's something you already know."

He pauses. I swallow.

"I'm in love with you—have been since eighth grade."

He looks into my eyes. My heart beats like it's trying to break out of my chest, but it all starts coming into focus like a Polaroid picture developing before my eyes.

If I'm honest with myself, I've been in love with Beau for a while, too. Why else would it bother me that he seemed indifferent to me? All of our fighting was just us fighting our attraction for each other. We were both stubborn and using Luke as an excuse.

"I'm in love with you, too," I whisper.

He leans down and puts his forehead to mine.

"I'm not going to kiss you tonight, Grace."

"You're not?"

Disappointment spirals down my chest.

"No. You've been through a lot today. Believe me. I want to kiss you, but I don't want to take advantage of you either."

A sense of gratitude washes over me for the kind of guy Beau is. I had almost wasted my first kiss on someone who couldn't have cared less about me.

Beau offers me his hand. I take it, this time understanding what the feeling was from before—love.

Epilogue

GRAMPS IS BACK IN THE pulpit, giving today's message. I snuggle next to Beau, the happiest I've been in a long time. Mr. and Mrs. Baron sit next to us in the pew. The only person missing is Bennett. He headed back to college after the last city's Watermelon Nectar release party with the excuse that he needed to get ready for the start of his semester. No one believes him. We all know he went early to spend time with Noelle, but we're not complaining.

Beau and I start our senior year in a couple of weeks, and while I'm not ready to go back to school, I am ready to start living again. I thought it was Warren that gave me the reason to be happy, but honestly, another person could never do that for me. The only way I can ever be truly happy is remembering what God did for me and giving my grief over to Him. If Beau hadn't tried to remind me of that in the old, red truck, who knows where I would be right now? Probably wallowing in self-pity.

Gramps closes his sermon and asks the choir to close us in singing. Beau and I share a hymnal and sing one of my favorites. His smooth baritone voice mixes with mine.

We all head over to the Barons' for Sunday dinner. Beau and I excuse ourselves as quickly as we can and jump in the old, red truck that Mr. Baron decided to have fixed instead of junking it. One of my favorite things to do with Beau is drive to all of our spots on the farm. Beau parks the truck by the pond and hurries around to get the door for me.

We walk for a while, and then we sit on a blanket that Beau brought.

"I can't believe the summer's almost over," I whine.

He leans back on his elbows and crosses his legs at the ankle.

"Me either."

"At least we still will have several promotions to go on. My year's only a third of the way done."

"True, but Mom seems to be a little more protective of you. She's not leaving us alone when you're in your crown and sash anymore."

"Hmmm, I wonder why that is," I tease him.

"I try to kiss you one time, and she walks in."

"You know the rules," I say.

But I don't really mean it. He's tried to kiss me only that one time, and I've been wondering when he'd try again.

He sits up.

"I have something for you."

He reaches in his back jeans pocket and pulls out a bracelet. It's silver and has a red truck charm and watermelon charm hanging from it.

"What's this?" I ask.

"So, I was going to give this to you in eighth grade, but I'm sure you know why I didn't."

"You've kept it this whole time?"

"Grace, I told you. You're the girl for me, and I've known for a really long time. It was only you that took some convincing."

"I know it now." I smile, holding out my hand to him.

He clips the bracelet on my wrist.

"It originally had just the watermelon charm on it. I just bought the red truck, seeing how it all started there."

He winks at me.

"The red truck, huh?" I don't even fight the smile spreading across my face.

"That night we ran in the rain. You were so beautiful. It was all I could think about while we ran."

I rub my finger over the red truck charm.

"Thanks, Beau. It's perfect."

He stands up, brushing off his hands, and then pulls me up beside him in a hug.

"I was thinking, we could add some charms to represent your family. We can go and pick them out tomorrow if you'd like."

It's just like Beau to know what's important to me and to think of a way to include my parents and Luke.

"I would like that a lot," I say as he leans toward me.

And in that moment, I know he's going to kiss me. Happiness washes over me when his lips touch mine. My first kiss may have been a long time coming, but it was so worth the wait.

Acknowledgments

First and foremost, thank you to my Lord and Savior Jesus Christ. Without Him nothing else matters. I count myself blessed that this process was part of the journey He had carved out for my life.

A BIG thank you goes out to my husband and my family for giving me the time I needed to write this story and for being my support team along the way.

To my Watermelon Family, thank you for a wonderful year full of amazing experiences and friendships to last a lifetime. I will always be grateful for the melon-sized memories that inspired this purely fictional story!

Thank you to A.B. and L.M. Your encouragement and joy for me throughout has been a blessing. T.L., thank you for being my sounding board and letting me talk it out when I needed to during brainstorming sessions. And, Nicole, thank you for always having my back, and being willing to jump in and help me reach my dream in any way you can.

Lastly, to you the reader, thank you for choosing to read this book, and stepping into the world of watermelons with me. I hope you enjoyed it!

For more information about

April Smith
and
Loving Grace
please visit:

www.aprilsmithbooks.com
@aprilsmithbook
www.facebook.com/aprilsmithbooks

For more information about
AMBASSADOR INTERNATIONAL
please visit:

www.ambassador-international.com
@AmbassadorIntl
www.facebook.com/AmbassadorIntl

If you enjoyed this book, please consider leaving us a review on
Amazon, Goodreads, or our website.

79625002R00126

Made in the USA
Middletown, DE
11 July 2018